BACK TO YOU

STARLIGHT HARBOR

BRIA QUINLAN

ALSO BY BRIA QUINLAN

BREW HA HA Series

It's In His Kiss (FREE Prequel)

The Last Single Girl

Worth the Fall

The Catching Kind

The Proposing Kind

Things That Shine - A Crossover Brew Ha Ha /Double Blind Story

Bria's YA set RVHS Secrets

Secret Girlfriend

Secret Life

And YA Standalone

Wreckless

BACK TO YOU

A prodigal daughter…

Vivian Breck left town years ago after she and her first love "took a break." With a not-so-secret baby on the way and a mother who was anything but understanding, she left Starlight Harbor to make sure her little one had nothing but love when he was born.

A first love never forgotten…

Camden Ross never got over losing Vi in high school and now that she's back, he'll do anything to win her—and her son—over. He's got family on the brain and there's only two people who can fill that hole in his heart.

Love never dies…

When the notorious Ms. Angie and her sidekick puppy Captain Jack Slickpaws wreck the town sleigh, Vivian needs work side-by-side with Cam to repair it before the next Starlight Harbor vintage weekend or risk losing the state heirloom to a museum who is threatening to play finders-keepers. With the town's history on the line, why is she having trouble focusing past the cut forearms woodworking first love?

WARNING: The Starlight Harbor series is a collection of quirky, fast-fall romances. You may start as enemies, but this novellete series means you'll end up as more -- Also, you'll have to battle the town lairds (yes, plural), a troublemaking pup, and the women who seem to think there's a 1900s war.

1

VIVIAN

VIVIAN BRECK only had room for one man in her life—and he was currently missing.

Vi set her wrench on the tool chest at the bottom of the stairs and strode up them and through the apartment over her garage one more time.

"Tyler?" Nothing came back but her own voice. "I am going to kill that boy. That's the only way I'll be able to stop worrying that someone else has killed him."

The only emotion bigger than how frustrated he often left her was how much she loved him.

A quick scan of their rooms told her he'd been home and had headed back out. Tyler was nine-going-on-twenty. She didn't care how many times they had to have the conversation. She'd drill it into his head he didn't have free run of Starlight Harbor if it was the last thing she did. His safety was the number one purpose in her life and a huge part of why she'd moved back to a place that had turned its back on her years ago.

Not just turned its back, but had out-and-out stood against her in some cases.

It wasn't like they lived in a bad section of a shady neighborhood in a huge, anonymous city. She could probably list not only the names but the phone numbers of every person he could have run into since baseball camp got out. But she'd been in those rough neighborhoods, and she knew there was just as much of a chance of bad things happening in sunny seaside towns as in places with bad reputations.

She was just about to call the rec center when she heard the buzz of a table saw and knew exactly where her son was.

Vi pulled the apartment door shut behind her with something stronger than the soft snick of a mother in complete control of her patience. She headed down the stairs, dropped the *Closed* sign on the office door, and tried not to storm through the shared area between her garage and the custom woodworking shop across the U-shaped space between their connected buildings.

Vi was on her fifth round of counting to ten before she pushed the door open, knowing what she'd find.

Inside, the table saw roared to life again, and she slowed her steps, afraid to accidentally cause her little man to chop his fingers off.

When she peeked around the corner, she saw Tyler standing on a small stool off to the side, a wooden horse and a lot of space between him and the Saw of Death. He leaned forward, trying to watch every move, every cut as Cam worked his magic.

The saw slowed and died again.

Cam slid the protective earplugs out of his ears and motioned for Tyler to remove the huge, super-duty earmuff-looking things that covered most of his head.

"Now, see how I held that? That's the first and most important thing. Safety."

"I thought it was measure twice, cut once." Her son's

voice sounded even smaller after the deep timbre of Cam's rumbling directions.

Cam laughed and pushed his protective eye gear up and looked Tyler straight in the eye. "Safety first, always. That's why you're not allowed in here or your mom's shop by yourself."

If Vi wasn't so stinking mad her son was exactly where he wasn't supposed to be—and with Camden Ross to boot—she'd be feeling pretty darn thankful to hear her own message being echoed back from another adult.

Her son mumbled something she was pretty sure would have had her saying "Excuse me?" in the patented Mom Voice.

"It isn't about trusting you," Cam went on patiently. "It's about training and the fact that all the tools both your mom and I use are fitted to adults, not smaller people. You'll grow into them."

Cam was handling the situation exactly right which made Vi want to roll her eyes for reasons she wasn't ready to discuss even with herself.

The fact Cam was handling *anything*—right or not—was just ticking her off. Now to figure out, while there were no sharp, pointy things being powered by electrical charges, exactly who she was more annoyed with.

"There you are." Vi stepped into the room and stared her son down, forcing herself not to let her gaze drift to her neighbor. "I'm confused. This isn't our apartment or the rec center, so this absolutely isn't where you were supposed to be."

Out of the corner of her eye, she caught Cam's head whip from her back to her son, a small frown on his face. He opened his mouth, then shut it.

Wise man.

Her son wasn't as smart.

"You said to come straight home from camp. And I did." It was funny how small his voice still sounded coming out of a body that was growing so quickly. She could have sworn those shorts were longer on him just last week.

No wonder so much of her budget went to food.

"This doesn't look like our living room." She stepped into the room, finally letting herself glance at Cam who had locked a neutral expression on his face.

It ticked her off—geez, everything was ticking her off today—that she couldn't at least partially blame this on him.

"I came home, put my stuff in my room, and *then* I came over here." Tyler was getting that stubborn tightness around the edges of his mouth she wished she could blame on his father. "The buildings are *attached*. I'm technically still home."

She wasn't sure if the noise Cam made was a snort or an exasperated sigh. Even he wasn't buying this, and she had firsthand experience with how stubborn he could be.

"Head up to your room. I'll be there in a minute."

She was pretty sure Tyler was considering a revolt. The fact he even looked in Cam's direction was something she'd file away for the conversation she and Tyler would be having later about who was the parent and who wasn't.

Her son stormed out of the workshop, preteen agony written all over every movement. She hadn't expected this for a few more years, but she'd known it was coming.

Of course, she didn't think he'd find his new hero right across their front yard... and certainly not that it would be Camden Ross of all people.

When she heard the outside door slam shut behind Tyler, she turned back to the man in the heavy leather apron and tried not to let the swirl of emotions overtake what needed to be said.

This wasn't the time to let the hormones of teenagers past step into the conversation.

Even if the man made an oversized leather apron look hot.

Before she could start, Cam raised a hand. "There's no need to say anything. I completely agree with you. And I hate to talk out of turn, but I asked him if you knew where he was when he came in. I'm sorry. I should probably learn to check with you or something."

Oh, so he was going to be all Mr. Reasonable and crap?

He knew how she hated that.

He was probably doing it just to annoy her.

Vi took a deep breath to even out the emotions she didn't want to be fighting. She was building a life for her and Tyler. That Cam was accidentally a part of the after... well, not being was a snag she hadn't fully anticipated.

"Cam, don't take this the wrong way, but I just don't think he should be over here at all." She waved a hand around at all the fairly deadly machinery making up Cam's custom woodworking studio and went on. "It's pretty dangerous in here. I know my garage is a safety issue as well, but I guess..."

"You're his mom." Cam shook his head, signaling that he got it. Moms had a different sense of awareness of their kids.

"And, well..." Vivian all but took a step back, not knowing how to phrase the next part. "It's just..."

Cam's gaze heated her skin like a beam of sunlight in an already hot room. He *had* to know what she was going to say. Was he really going to make her spell it out?

Apparently, he was.

"With our history—"

"Wait, really?" Cam interrupted.

"Yes. Really." She charged ahead, not giving him a chance to break in again. "With our history, I don't think it's healthy for Tyler to be over here, running back and forth between our houses as if he were allowed free rein."

"Okay, first of all." Cam literally took off the gauntlets for this as he stripped the heavy leather gloves from his hands and tossed them aside. "He doesn't have free rein. He knows there are rules to being in the workshop. And secondly, how long are you going to hold that against me?"

"I'm not holding anything against you. I'm just saying that letting Tyler create a close bond with you is probably a bad idea."

"Because of our history," he drawled sarcastically.

Vivian wasn't willing to be sucked into a circular argument. This wasn't the time or place, and her son certainly wasn't the reason.

"Yes."

Cam gave her a long, hard stare. One she was all too familiar with. And then, before she knew what was happening, he stepped into her space, forcing her to look up at him as few men could from her own height even without her work boots.

"I made a mistake when I was sixteen. I was stupid, which is par for the course. I'll take my share of the blame for anything you want to call 'our history.' But know this, Vivian. I never stopped loving you. I was stupid to think it wasn't love then, but I'm not too stupid to know what it is now."

2

CAM

AS SOON AS the words left his mouth, he regretted them.

He'd held them in for over a year since she'd moved back and he couldn't believe he let them just rush out of his mouth in an angry tirade like that.

Not his smoothest move.

Of course, he'd been holding them longer than a year if he was being honest—and apparently, he suddenly was.

Being honest, that was.

He'd known as soon as he'd broken up with her that he was an idiot. But he figured, what the hell? It wasn't like they wouldn't get back together after they both dated a few people. They were young. It would make them more solid for the long run if they went out a couple times here and there with other people.

And small towns were famous for the whole matchmaking-at-birth crap. His teen self had been tired of hearing about weddings and babies.

He'd been sixteen for heaven's sake.

Then—

"I'm not blaming you." Vi broke into his thoughts,

completely redirecting the conversation back to "their past" but away from "I love you." He watched her lock down the walls of denial between them. "Even if I did, I got Tyler from that time. But I need to draw a line. And you being the dad he wants, doesn't mean you're the dad he gets."

Cam hated that she was right. Hated things were always going to be so layered between them.

He hated that this hurt her—and because he knew her better than any other human, he could see the hurt behind her tough exterior.

An exterior he was partly to blame for, not that she hadn't always had a bit of a tough-girl attitude. It was one thing he'd loved about her even when he didn't understand it.

Besides, Cam wasn't a man who needed to have layers in his life. He had a family he loved and who loved him. He had a career in a field he was gifted in which allowed him to make beautiful things and sell them while feeding himself. He had good friends, a good life, a nice home.

He just didn't have Vivian.

He took a deep breath before going on knowing she'd see him in the wrong no matter what.

"I'm not trying to butt in. Vi, I asked him straight out." He was repeating himself but he wasn't sure what else to do.

He felt like he'd been repeating himself for almost a decade.

Of course, that whole shouting-he-loved-her thing was new.

Definitely not how he wanted to add layers.

"I just—" She took a step back and he knew she was already out the door. They weren't even going to talk about this. "I just need you to realize there are boundaries that have to stay in place and you need to respect them."

Cam shoved his frustration back because she was right.

This wasn't just about letting Tyler over to his workshop for lessons. He *wanted* Tyler there. He wanted Vivian there too.

"I get that. But, Vivian, Tyler is curious and talented. I enjoy his company. I hope you don't think I'm overstepping, but I think he enjoys being around a guy who isn't trying to push him. I'm not a coach or a teacher—or a dad. I'm just the guy who lives on the other side of the bailey."

He glanced out the window at their rooms overlooking the same space, a flash of pain shooting through his gut.

He'd wondered, of course he'd wondered.

First when she disappeared before they could even start senior year, then over the years as he couldn't help but wonder about her and her baby. Every day for half a decade, he expected to turn a corner and see her there, all long-legged beauty and auburn-haired sass.

When she came back, Tyler in tow, she was more than his sixteen-year-old self could have foreseen and all that a full-grown man could want in a woman.

Funny, smart, strong, loyal... and gorgeous, she was still gorgeous.

He shouldn't have been surprised when the woman who was all those things wasn't having him anywhere near the lines she'd drawn on the ground.

"He has men in his life," she insisted. As if that were the only thing he'd said. As if she was latching on to the easiest thing to address.

"I didn't say he didn't, but guys need different types of men. No one can be everyone to anyone."

"Don't I know it." She gave him a look, accusing him of having dropped that ball for her already.

"I was sixteen. Vivian, I thought we'd come back to each other after not being together for a few weeks. It was stupid, but I was feeling hedged in. I didn't expect..."

That *she'd* start seeing someone right away. His stupid teen brain had assumed he'd go out with a few girls who flirted with him regularly, see what that was like, then be the big guy on campus who graciously took her back.

Because, again, idiot.

"Didn't expect I'd get pregnant?" Vivian's irate voice broke into his thoughts.

Cam was taken off guard by the anger in her voice.

"What? No," he insisted as he struggled to align what he'd been thinking with what she'd just said. "I didn't expect you to *leave*."

He paced away, running a hand through his hair, tempted to yank it out at the roots.

Is that what she thought of him?

Sure, he'd been ticked off. They'd been waiting. He'd been ready to wait forever for her when it came to sex. And not in a pushy way.

His dad had sat him down when he was twelve and said, "Ever want to play a game with someone who didn't want to play but you guilted them into it? How much fun was that?"

Then came the sex talk.

He never wanted to be that guy.

Especially with Vivian because she was special. She'd always been special.

"You were there and then you were just—gone." He turned back to look at her. "How do you fix stuff with someone who just left?"

"Oh, and you couldn't find me?" The snark was real. And the pain. He had to wonder how much that accusation weighted this conversation.

Cam felt like he was still stuck on repeat. "Again, I was sixteen. And an idiot. I feel like these two facts keep coming up and are given no weight. I mean, the idiocy of sixteen-year-old boys is extremely well-documented."

Like in every way possible.

"You're really using 'I was an idiot' as your go-to defense?" Vivian looked like she was about to blow a gasket instead of fix one.

"And then what?" Cam demanded, looking back at the past with eyes as clear as he could manage. Even as he said it, he remembered the truth. The one that still haunted him. "I find you and then you... come back and we go to prom? You *left*. I screwed up, but you left."

Vivian stepped back, her face going blank, but not before she locked down the anger that flashed in her eyes first, a storm of green on gold.

"You know what? I don't have time for this. I have a nine-year-old at home planning a revolt. I'd appreciate it if you'd send him home next time he shows up here."

She turned to go and Cam saw everything from the past and the present slamming into one another again like a flash over of pictures where there should have just been one.

"Vivian, wait." He tensed, as if this moment were the only chance he had. She stood, her back to him, and he added, "Can we talk about this?"

Her shoulders sagged as her head dropped back in defeat that nearly killed him before she braced and turned around, the same Valkyrie he was used to.

"About what?"

Cam wanted to say all of it, but he knew it wouldn't

lead him anywhere helpful. It wasn't like repeating everything for the three hundred and fifty seventh time would change anything.

But there were other things he wanted.

He *enjoyed* Tyler. And not just because his sassy nine-year-old self was a mini-me of his mom at that age.

The kid had potential, a great eye, and made Cam laugh like no one outside of his guys.

He saw himself losing yet another Breck because of something he'd done a decade ago when he was a stupid teenage boy. Which was apparently going to need to be printed on all his t-shirts now:

I Blame Teenage Me

Before Vivian could lay down more laws than he could navigate, he rushed on. "I'd like to mentor Tyler. He's talented and interested. You of all people know we're lucky we have a skill and a trade. I'd like to make sure if he's able and stays interested, he'll have that too if it's what he wants."

He knew he was on the right track. The other conversation would not have brought him where he wanted and he was going to have to live with that.

For now.

"And you'd make the rules," he continued. "Because, honestly, I have zero interest in being the kid's patsy."

"Again." Vivian finally broke out in a grin.

"What?"

"You have zero interest in being his patsy *again*."

Cam grinned. There she was. His sassy girl.

"I wouldn't mind being your patsy." He laughed as she turned, trying to hide her smirk and strode out of his workshop.

3
_____

VIVIAN

VIVIAN WAS TRYING NOT to feel tag-teamed as she headed across the yard to have a talk with Tyler. She worked to shake off the feeling that Cam had gotten exactly what he wanted, even though her son had invited himself over and then she'd stormed his workshop ready to throw down.

It was hard to admit to herself Cam wasn't in the wrong here.

She'd spent a lot of years blaming him for a lot of things —and sure, he deserved a huge chunk of that. But she had her fair share of blame to take as well.

But when she looked around her life now, what was the point of blame? She had her friends. She had her home. And best of all, she had Tyler.

She and Cam had been kids, both of them stupid in the way only someone with high emotions and low life experience could be.

Now they were adults and she liked her life—no, she *flipping loved* her life. Since she and Tyler had moved back to Starlight Harbor, things had been better than she could have hoped for. She'd used the money she'd gotten from selling the garage Charlie had left her and moved home.

She hadn't realized Starlight Harbor was home when she'd been gone. She hadn't longed for it or thought she'd missed it. But as soon as she crossed the town line when she'd returned to bury her mother, she'd known she'd be moving her and Tyler back for good.

She'd been braced for the judgment and the whispers. But people had mostly just nodded and moved on with a small welcome.

Starlight Harbor was in her soul like only a generational, small town could be.

It was home.

And now she was braced for a different type of battle: the one dealing with her son.

She was almost to the front door when a car flew into the drive, beeping at her as it did.

"Vivian! Thank goodness I found you." Ms. Angie was jumping out of her car, parked haphazardly across the edge of the drive. "It's an emergency and no one can fix it but you."

Vi glanced up at the living room window, figuring it would serve Tyler right to be stuck inside for a few more minutes while she helped Ms. Angie with whatever this week's emergency was.

"Ms. Angie, I thought the town council said no more driving on city streets for you." She shook her head as she headed toward the elderly lady, knowing no matter what the council told her, it would take an accident or an act of God to keep her from getting behind the wheel.

And it was only a fifty-fifty she'd listen to either.

Stealing her car had been suggested several times before her Speed Racer routine got someone—or something—hurt.

Today she had on a corset with skull and crossbones running down the edging. Her sidekick, Captain Jack Slickpaws, a four-legged troublemaker, wore a matching bandana.

"It's the sleigh, dear." Ms. Angie shook her head and Vi was suddenly worried she'd tried to drive the town's classic sleigh herself.

This was far, far more serious than she'd expected.

As a town that celebrated Christmas for servicemen and women and their families every two to three weeks, if something had happened to Santa's sleigh, the whole town would be up in arms.

And stealing Ms. Angie's car would be the least of the suggestions.

Instead of panicking, Vi just pasted a smile on her face and gave her a *don't worry* look. "I'm sure it's nothing we can't handle. What happened to the sleigh?"

Vivian ignored the obvious question of what Ms. Angie was doing with the sleigh. But really, a person could only take so much craziness at once.

"Well, it's really quite remarkable. We were polishing the wood along the edges when Captain Jack jumped into the car and released the emergency brake—quite by accident of course—and before you know it, he—and it—were rolling forward. And I'll be a smuggler's peg leg, but I couldn't jump over the door to get in to stop it—and long story medium, we crashed the sleigh."

"Oh, my." Vivian was suddenly not feeling as light and fluffy about this accident.

And really, Captain Jack? How in the world had Ms. Angie's twelve-pound pup—breed unknown—released the parking brake?

She opened her mouth to ask just that when she realized she was probably better off not knowing. Ms. Angie most likely had a very long, very detailed dramedy to explain it.

"How bad of a crash are we talking?"

"Well..." Ms. Angie glanced away, the guilt level flushing her cheeks leaving Vi to worry that the thing would need to be rebuilt from scratch. "The front end is kind of dinged."

"Dinged, dented, or smashed in?"

"Maybe closer to the third," the older lady admitted.

This wasn't going to be fixed with a quick drive-by and some jumper cables.

"Okay, give me five minutes and I'll meet you over at the town barn."

She hated letting Ms. Angie get behind the wheel alone, but as a single mom, there was no way she was getting in there with her.

Plus, she still had to deal with Tyler.

Which was going to be more of a To Be Continued situation than she would have liked.

Heading upstairs, she went through the door to find him in his beanbag chair with a book in his hand and his Thor action figure sitting on his shoulder as if reading along. If he had set himself up to look adorable and like a son who didn't break rules explicitly laid out for him, he'd done a good job.

But she wasn't going to be dissuaded that easily.

"Tyler." She waited until he looked up. Books were the only thing she let him have leeway on. No one wanted to have to stop reading in the middle of a book—er, a sentence. "Ms. Angie was just here and needs my help. I'll be down at the town barn. You have two options, come with or stay here. Period. No in-between or bartering."

He glanced toward the window, obviously thinking

neither sounded great with the sun shining and summer barely in full swing.

"You lost the outside option and you know why. Also, the two of us have an appointment for a family meeting at dinner, so don't think you're off the hook on that either."

Tyler settled back in his chair, crossing his arms.

"Fine. I'll stay here." He hurried on as she grabbed her wallet and phone. "Can me and Thor read on the roof deck?"

Since she'd put high railings up there, he'd been asking all the time, but that was a no go. "No. You know you can't be on the roof without an adult."

"How about Cam?"

Vivian mentally counted to ten at warp speed since she needed to be somewhere. "Cam has to work, and you already got him in trouble, which we will be talking about."

She ignored the heavy sigh from her offspring as she headed toward the door. If anyone should be tossing out deep sighs, it was her. He was way too young to be acting this difficult. There was no way she'd last through another decade of this.

There were going to be some serious resetting of rules and boundaries tonight.

Tyler was going to find out what happens when you lie to an adult, lie to your mom, and break a standing rule pretending it was a loophole.

And he wasn't going to like it.

Vi was halfway across town when she realized she'd forgotten to let Cam know Tyler was on lockdown since her trust level in her son was running at nil. But Cam wasn't an idiot. She had to trust he'd get that if he saw her little guy wander in.

Pulling into the town buildings' parking lot, she couldn't

help but notice the crowd gathering behind the large barn they stored the Christmas Holidayer's things in.

"Oh, look. The cavalry." Mrs. Macalister, her fourth-grade teacher, grinned at her as Vivian came striding across the parking lot. "Vivian, you are not going to like what you see here."

"How bad is it?" she asked, pulling out her travel toolbox and iPhone to get some decent pictures of the damage.

"How bad? Maybe leave the toolbox and bring the tow truck?"

Vivian shook her head, trying not to roll her eyes as people glanced their way. "Only Ms. Angie."

"I think you mean only Ms. Angie's dog. You know she'll never take the blame for this."

"Truer words."

The two women headed toward the crowd as Ms. Angie flitted around, answering questions that weren't going to get anything moving.

"Oh, Vivian. Thank goodness you're here," she gushed as if she hadn't just been at Vi's shop to get her.

"Okay, Ms. Angie. Let's see what Captain Jack did this time."

The crowd parted and Vivian stutter-stepped to a halt, nearly dropping her toolbox at the same time.

"Ms. Angie!" She turned toward the older woman, shocked at the understatement of damage she'd made. "The sleigh needs more than a little tweaking. I don't even know..."

She went around to the front of the motorized sleigh and just stared. The front end was completely smashed in. There was as much body damage if not more than a fender bender would have created. Gently unlatching what was left of the front of the sleigh, she lifted it away and found a mass of engine wreckage under the hood.

"Well?" Ms. Angie stood next to her, looking down at what was obviously a destroyed engine.

"All I can say is I hope Captain Jack has insurance." She pulled on some work gloves, ignoring the gaffs from the crowd. "It looks like we're going to need to get this into the shop. This isn't a quicky job you've got here."

Behind her a small yip grabbed her attention.

"Sure, Captain Jack. You give all the advice you want, but it's not going to get you out of trouble."

"So, you can have it done by the next Holiday, right?" Ms. Angie was starting to sound nervous.

Which she absolutely should. This was ridiculous. Vivian would have to be a miracle worker to get the sleigh ready for the next Holidayer's weekend in sixteen days.

Grabbing her flashlight, she leaned under the hood and checked out the frame to see if there was any structural damage. Looking good on the outside was great, but safety was vital—especially since you never knew who would be working the sleigh. It wasn't a private vehicle with an owner who could deal with small quirks if they chose to.

Next, she was on her back and scooting under. There was a potential crack in the axle, but it looked like some old wear that would have gone soon anyway, sans Captain Jack's big adventure.

Still, it would have to be replaced.

Vi turned the flashlight off and just lay there under the cool undercarriage, not ready to face the hopeful crowd above her.

"Well?" Ms. Angie shouted as if she had gone into another room, not just lay on the ground.

"Well." Vivian scooted back out, wiping her hands

down her jumpsuit pants as she did. "It's not pretty. I don't think we can get this done quickly. I mean, I'm not even sure how I'll handle the bodywork. The list of potential issues is long at just a glance."

The group who had been cracking themselves up with sleigh puns fell silent.

Santa's sleigh was a big deal in these parts. It was one of the symbols of Christmas they kept out in an obvious way— the one true kitschy thing they did was have Santa drive through town for any active Christmas weekend.

They'd also had a bride arrive to the church in it, the new town manager driven to their inauguration, and a few other local events.

Let's just put it this way, renting the sleigh wasn't cheap and that kept the wear and tear down.

Obviously, Captain Jack hadn't filled out any rental forms or waivers.

And it wasn't like they could move Holiday weekends. She'd seen the schedule. They had a military family of nearly twenty people coming in fourteen days—eight of those were kids under twelve.

Not that they needed kids to be involved.

Any reason to crack the sleigh out was a good one.

Of course, this isn't how they had wanted it cracked.

Ms. Angie glanced down at the sleigh and then smiled. "Don't worry about the bodywork. I made a call."

That was something. Vivian wasn't sure who Ms. Angie knew who had "professional sleigh repairman" on their résumé, but it was better than her trying to figure out how to bend wood like that.

"I'm going to need to go get the wrecker."

"Oh, dear! No. We don't want to wreck it!" Ms. Angie

threw her body in front of the sleigh. "Fix it, dear. We want to fix it."

"I know, ma'am. Don't worry. The wrecker is just what they call the tow truck I'm going to bring back." Vivian was packing up her tools, ready to head home and finish the day's work—not to mention have a heart-to-heart with Tyler and figure out if she could really trust him in a woodworking shop.

And if she wanted to trust him with Cam.

"Great." Ms. Angie gave her a bright smile. "I'll wait here."

Vi stopped as she pushed the tool kit into the back of her truck.

"What do you mean, stay here?"

"Well, you've got to come back and I want to hear about the plan and stuff too."

Vivian glanced around and realized the entire town was not going to take no for an answer. She was a single mom, with a full load at her garage already. She had no idea where she'd find the time.

If the town really wanted the sleigh done pronto, some of them were going to have to live without their cars for a bit.

She glanced up at the sky, wondering how she was going to fit in more time with Tyler—which was obviously a must since he'd decided listening was optional—and keep on her client schedule while making it all work together.

It was all adding up around her as she stood in the bright sunshine, a dead sleigh resting on the deader tree stump behind her with the town looking on as if she were Wonder Woman.

"Well, now. It's not every day I'm asked to work as an elf to Santa."

She should have known who the sleigh fixer was. It was stupid in retrospect not to, but her day had been spiraling from the second she woke up—missing sons, ridiculous, uncalled for I love yous, sleigh-crashing dog drivers.

Vi glanced up to see Cam standing at the edge of the crowd, arms crossed as he stared at the smashed-in wood and metal, before his gaze slid her way and he gave her a quick wink.

"I mean, accidents happened, but really, Ms. Angie." He shook his head at the older woman. "Letting Captain Jack drive is just above and beyond. Even for you."

For the first time since she'd gotten there, Ms. Angie seemed to relax a bit.

"Camden, you scoundrel. It wasn't Captain Jack's fault. It wasn't like we were out and about."

Vivian couldn't help but wonder exactly what they were doing that the dog had access to the emergency brake, but she held her tongue. This didn't all add up to "just polishing the sleigh" to her.

Since Ms. Angie had learned about selfies, she'd been completely out of control.

"Let's see what we've got here." He strode toward the sleigh, his dark gaze clashing with Vivian's for just an instant as he gave her a nod. "Vivian."

She watched, ignoring the way his jeans stretched over his rear as he did the same checks she'd just done herself, but on the damage to the woodwork along the front end and the cracking he found at the sides.

Part of her heart ached for him. Motors could be replaced, but this work... she could tell by the look he kept faced away from Ms. Angie and the way his hand gently caressed the broken angles and shattered pieces of wood that this was more personal than just the ability to drop in a new transmission.

When he straightened, he took a moment to clear his expression before turning to face their audience.

"Ms. Angie, really. This sleigh was built by Raymond Havester. His work is incomparable. I can only try to repair this in a way that respects the original. It isn't like changing a light bulb and the Tiffany lamp still shines the same."

The older lady flinched and Vivian only had so much sympathy for her. Like the rest of the town, she loved Ms. Angie. But the woman ran tame through everything and now she'd obviously gone a step too far.

The humor of the situation was beginning to wear off of the crowd too and Vivian was pretty sure if either she or Cam called the job impossible, there might be a revolt.

She wanted Ms. Angie to know she'd created a bad situation with her lack of care, not be tarred and feathered.

"Show's over, folks." Vivian clapped her hands, trying to dispel the group.

Just when she thought they'd ignore her, Skye, best friend number two and deputy sheriff, stepped through the crowd, following her example.

"That's enough lollygagging as Ms. Angie would say. I'm sure you all"—she glanced around, giving some pointed looks—"or most of you, have work you should be doing. Let Vivian and Cam do theirs."

She didn't want to wait to see who fought the law since the law would win. Instead, Vivian headed back to her truck, not wanting to face either Cam or her own worry about how she'd fix... well, everything.

Especially when "everything" included Camden Ross.

4

CAM

WHEN HE'D BLURTED out his undying love that morning, Cam hadn't thought the day could get weirder... or worse.

But seeing the Raymond Havester work caved in because of a freaking dog just about pushed him over the edge.

That sleigh was the reason he did what he did. Every time they had taken it out when he was a boy, he found a detail on it that fascinated him, from the scroll work along the edges to the dipped runners that hid the wheels, and especially the little elves hidden in cracks and crevices peeking out all the way around.

The thing was more than a work of art. It was a national treasure and should be protected. The artist in him battled between "someone should call the National Register" and "functional art was made to be used."

As soon as he had understood someone made this—that this was what they did for a living—everything had changed. First, he'd started asking for books on whittling like Mr. Crocker did down on the pier. Then knives—which his mother had absolutely no-go'd until he was nine. Then he'd discovered the library.

The library may not be where his friends expected to find him—that would have been the baseball field—but it had books filled with pictures of artisans' work going back centuries.

He'd known, just absolutely known, these guys didn't half-ass their way into these books. His mother had been more pleased, not to mention obscenely relieved, when the next thing he asked for was a sketch pad and some decent pencils.

He'd drawn everything he could think of to get the feel of it. Nothing was sacred. If the girl sitting next to him in fourth grade wanted flowers and bunnies, he asked what kind of flowers.

But it was the sleigh he came back to over and over again.

He'd drawn that sucker from every angle imaginable. Close-ups, distance draws, on the move, full glances and tight in on details—he'd even done the undercarriage a couple times.

It had been a dream of his to someday do something as magnificent and meaningful as it.

Raymond Havester hadn't just designed and built it, he'd painted it too.

Which of course Cam found out in sixth grade and, yes, asked for paints.

When he'd come around the corner and through the crowd, he'd been momentarily stunned by the wreckage. He'd had a good mind to let Vivian give Ms. Angie the scolding she was obviously working up to.

Thank God Skye had shown up with her deputy's hat on and thrown everyone out. He'd felt like he needed a minute, like there was some time of mourning that should be done for this living piece of art that would never be the same.

"You too, Ms. Angie. Let Vivian go get her truck and Camden do some assessing."

"But I'm sure we can help."

Cam straightened, about to tell her she'd done more than enough, when a hand landed softly on his back.

"We won't let her rush us. You'll have it good as new."

He glanced down at Vivian's upturned face, the wide deep-green eyes rimmed by dark-red lashes.

He'd thought she'd be ignoring him as much as possible, locking him out of her and Tyler's life after this morning. But here she was making sure he was pulling it together.

Cam gave her a quick nod and turned around, his face clear of all the anger he'd been fighting off for the last ten minutes.

"Ms. Angie. We have a lot of work to do, so Skye is right. You should move on so we can get started."

"And you'll have it done by the Holidayer's weekend?" she asked, obviously worried about taking the blame for a Santa-free parade this month.

Cam took a deep breath, trying not to use it to scream the top of his head off, and smiled at her. Taking Ms. Angie's arm, he walked her toward the entrance where her car was still parked—in one piece—an unrepentant Captain Jack sat waiting for her.

"You just head on home and let us do our thing. It will be done as quickly as we can get it there."

He watched as she buckled herself in before she and Captain Jack tore out of the yard like it was the start of the Indy 500, hell on wheels at eighty-two.

The brake lights barely flashed as she made the turn onto Main Street and Cam let his eyes drop shut.

"One day I'm just going to have to straight-out arrest that woman." Skye sighed as she turned back to Cam. "Vivian escaped to get her wrecker. I know this is a lot of pressure. Don't let them all get to you."

"Right." Cam turned, giving the sleigh his entire attention.

There'd be pictures and video galore, but he doubted any of it would show as much detail as he needed.

He pulled his cell from his back pocket and listened as it rang twice before an excited voice answered.

"Camden, you didn't cut yourself in half or lose a hand, did you?"

One of the top wood artists in the country, and his mother still expected him to spill blood daily.

"I'm fine, Mom. Everything's still where it should be." He stared hard at the sleigh as he circled it, making a note of even the few small damages along the side where he's pretty sure Ms. Angie did not admit to it grazing something on its careening race out of the barn. "Do you still have my sketchbooks from when I was a kid?"

"Of course!" She sounded shocked he even needed to ask. "I'd never throw out your things."

He didn't argue that his baseball jersey she'd donated years ago also counted.

"You don't mind if I come by later today and grab several?"

"Camden, this will always be your home."

He was pretty sure for most parents it was just a thing they said when kids wanted anything short of moving back in.

"You'll stay for dinner."

He should have known.

"A quick one. We're having a bit of an emergency."

His mother laughed and he was pretty sure she would have swatted him if he'd been there. "Oh, Camden. Who has a woodworker's emergency?"

He heaved a sigh. Sadly, he would have thought the same thing a day ago.

"That would be Starlight Harbor since Ms. Angie crashed the sleigh."

There was stunned silence on the other end before he heard the delayed gasp.

"That woman is a nuisance. And not just because of the sleigh. That sleigh is part of our history—and you love that thing. There were days I'd wished you'd never seen it."

He could only imagine.

"You come by for whatever you need," she continued. "I'll have a quick dinner for tonight and let your dad know there's not a game on the TV until you leave."

5

VIVIAN

"LYRA, YOU'RE A GODDESS! SAVE ME!" Vivian had dropped off the wrecker and the sleigh at town hall and did what any sane woman who was having child troubles, work troubles, and apparently man troubles would do: She ran to get some caffeine and a check-in with a bestie.

The door hadn't even fallen shut behind her when Lyra pointed to a small table with a coffee and two muffins sitting on it.

Lyra was smart enough to know neither of those muffins were for her, but she brought a tea with her as she sat across from Vivian.

"I heard Ms. Angie has really done it this time."

Vivian shook her head. She needed the caffeine and sugar before even pretending to address this.

Lyra just sat, waved at people who walked by the window, and sipped her tea. There were probably a million things she needed to be doing, but since Spence was still getting all his online-work-life stuff back on track, Vi was going to pretend her friend was completely free for any type of breakdown she needed to have.

"Skye may actually arrest her this time." Vi nodded toward the muffin. "Little early for cranberries, isn't it?"

"Nova Scotia."

"Ah." She took another bite, happy for Nova Scotia, and went on, "The sleigh is a mess, Lyra. I'm only saying that in this room with no other humans and reasonably assured no one has listening devices. I thought Cam was either going to cry or throttle her."

"Which was it?"

"Cry, I think. You should have seen how many deep breaths that man took before he turned around with his typical sunny, charming smile on his face."

"Charming, huh?"

Vi rolled her eyes. "You know he's charming. *He* knows he's charming. The whole darn town knows he's charming."

"Uh-huh." Lyra took a sip of her tea. "And good-looking. The whole town knows he's good-looking, too."

"Sure." Vi just shook her head because she knew she wasn't going to win this one. "Good-looking. I mean, that's subjective."

"And he's just nice, you know?" Lyra glanced toward the window, but Vi could feel her friend watching her out of the corner of her eye.

"Okay, what's going on?"

Lyra put her tea down and pushed it aside, leaning across the table. "Spence is convinced Cam is still in love with you and he's going to woo you and win you back like some knight of old."

Vi closed her eyes and leaned back, trying to ignore the goose bumps that ran down her arm.

Of course everyone would see it but her. She'd been so busy trying to block him out that she wouldn't notice any ideas he might have been getting.

It made sense though. Cam was a competitive sort and a romantic. You put those together and the fact he'd broken up with her in high school—and everything that came after that—of course he'd feel a deep and lasting need to win her back. In his mind, to put things right.

It didn't mean anything really, but she wasn't going to play it through.

His parents had basically met in the womb and had the perfect marriage.

And were just plain awesome anyway.

Across the table, Lyra cleared her throat.

"He's not," Vivian finally said. "Or at least he's not in the way I'm sure Mr. Romantic thinks he is. Dude was born in the wrong century."

"Seeing as I was an eyewitness to both of you in your teen years in this very century"—Lyra cocked an eyebrow at her—"I'm going to have to strongly disagree with everything you just said."

"I didn't come here to get lectured about my love life—"

"Lack of."

"I came here to get sustenance to deal with that hot wreck they're taking pictures of behind town hall before I haul it back to my place. You *know* this is going to turn into A Thing."

Lyra nodded. That's why she'd put out not one, but two muffins. Even if it killed her a little that Vivian could eat all she wanted and she could only taste her own creations.

"Let's be honest, it already is. If I hadn't promised Spence I'd stay off social media and all things that allow any type of comments while he was out of town, I'd be all over the place watching the insanity."

Just as she finished, the door burst open and one of the Proctor twins rushed in. "OH MY GOSH! Did you hear?"

She knew it had to be Kelsey because she was the twin trying to win her job back after getting let go for what was technically job abandonment—and not so technically Lyra being just done with her mother.

As soon as she saw Vivian, her face fell. "Well, I guess you have."

Instead of giving up, she walked in and joined them at the table. "Ms. Vi, any comment?" she asked, as she pulled out her phone.

"Comment?"

"Yeah." Kelsey perked up, a bright smile on her face. "I'm trying to get a top spot at *The Starlighter* this fall, and if I can get the scoop from you before anyone else, maybe that will put me ahead of Brian."

Vivian struggled because she was all about girl power, but she didn't have anything currently quotable for the high school paper.

"Okay, how 'bout this?" Vivian glanced in Lyra's direction, ignoring the complete amusement on her face. "At this time, expert engine technician—"

"Oh, that's good." Lyra laughed as she watched Kelsey type as quickly as possible.

"Thank you. Technician," she continued, "Vivian Breck cannot give a specific diagnosis of the sleigh's mechanical issues until a time when she can examine it in depth. But she can confirm there was some level of damage done to the town sleigh this morning. The town manager's office is visually recording the damage before handing the sleigh over to have the engine reviewed."

"That sounds very professional." Lyra wiggled her brows at her.

"Ms. Vi, would you mind if I follow up with you later? I'm going to do a preliminary post on my Facebook page."

"Of course. Come on over and I'll give you whatever I'm at liberty to."

"Awesome!" Kelsey made a bunch of notes before looking up again. "Do you think the town manager will give me a statement?"

Lyra snorted and Vivian couldn't help but snort on the inside.

"I think you might have more luck with Deputy Skye who was on the scene and Camden Ross who will be reviewing the woodworking."

"I love D-Skye. She gives the girls self-defense classes every year and she's killer."

Before either of the ladies could comment, Kelsey was up and out the door, shouting *thanks* over her shoulder.

They both sat there, taking in the craziness.

"You know that's just the start, right?" Lyra looked at her with sympathy. "I now recognize when crazy is coming for you, and, honey... it has you in its sights."

"Why isn't it coming for Ms. Angie?" She couldn't help but whine a bit. "This isn't my doing."

"Oh, sweetie." Lyra shook her head in sympathy. "It came for Ms. Angie decades ago and realized it might win the battle but would lose the war. That woman would out-bonkers the devil himself."

Before Vivian could decide just how much she agreed with that sentiment, her phone beeped.

"Town manager's office. Apparently, they want to talk. I hate talking. I just want to bring this thing to the garage and get it on a lift."

"Poor Vi. People wanting her to be social and stuff."

Vivian swept her crumbs onto her plate and stood to stack everything in the bus bin.

"Lyra, just because people like you—people being me—

doesn't mean they're above soaping your windows in spite for some things you might say."

Before Lyra could make a response, Vi was out the door, thrilled to get in the last word with someone today.

6

CAM

CAM WALKED the four blocks to his parents' house, glad for the thinking time.

This had to work. He hadn't realized he even had a plan when he made his plan. Maybe he'd been considering this for a month. Or years.

But he had realized after she left, it was Vivian or nothing. He knew there was no way he could stay here—especially sharing a yard with them—if he couldn't be more than just her neighbor or friend. He kept trying to keep his mind on the problem at hand—the sleigh—but his heart kept deciding its problem was more important and taking over.

By the time he got to his childhood house, he had if not a plan, a desperate idea to set into action. He had not only a need to make this work, but an opportunity to spend time with Vi—try to win her back—and there was nothing she could do about it.

He didn't even have to kidnap her or anything.

Not that he'd considered that.

Well, crap. When did he become a stalker? She was the one who had moved into his bailey. Jamie had accused him after she moved back to Starlight Harbor of buying that building for his shop and apartment because of the garage. If she ever came back, of course she'd need a garage.

Cam wasn't stupid. He hadn't consciously made that decision, but once Jamie said it, he couldn't help but wonder if he had done it subconsciously. When Lyra had finally shared where Vivian was and what she was doing, he'd found himself pondering it often. Then, two years later, there she was.

Of course, there weren't a lot of spaces like what he needed for his shop and it allowed him to walk wherever he wanted.

Justify, justify, justify.

By the time he'd convinced himself he had been given this chance to win back Vivian by fate, he was walking up his parents' front walk and wondering if he should send Captain Jack a special biscuit for arranging a second chance at his best future.

And also a stern talking-to about touching art.

"Hello, Frank." He gave the cat a scrub before letting the door fall shut. Fat Frank, his mother's cat, barking at him as he did.

He'd make a million bucks overnight if he'd just get a barking cat Instagram going, but his mother wanted to "protect Frank's dignity."

"Camden, honey. Don't annoy the cat." He glanced to where she was transplanting some of her herbs into outside containers. They'd had a late frost and he was sure she was feeling that with her garden still.

He rounded the table and kissed her on the cheek before checking out the cookie jar next to the sun tea pitcher.

BACK TO YOU   37

"You're so predictable." She grinned as he chomped down on a peanut butter chip oatmeal cookie.

"And you made my favorite because I called ahead."

"I have to keep busy during the summer. It's amazing how much more energy I have when I'm not trying to keep fourteen-year-olds' attention while discussing Shakespeare and how relevant he is to them."

"I loved your Shakespeare."

She snorted. Fourteen wasn't so long ago she didn't remember how horrible he'd been at English Lit.

"Your dad brought down the boxes that were in the attic and put them in your room. Just the ones you have in those special crates with your sketch pads." She washed her hands off and turned around. "You have about two hours till dinner, and then if you need us to drive you back with them, we can do that, or you can just come back tomorrow. You're always—"

"Welcome here. I know, Ma." He gave her a bright grin.

Those had been her ongoing words since Vivian had left home.

He doubted she even remembered when she started saying it, but he knew the exact date.

Vivian had gotten pregnant like five minutes after they broke up. There were rumors going around it was his. Which made sense because of how close the dates of breakup to pregnancy were. And he didn't argue with it because if she needed it to be his, it was.

Period.

But then her mother had started publicly attacking Vivian and threatening to kick her out. And his mother had been acting all... motherish.

Finally, he came home one night and his parents were

both waiting for him in the kitchen, each with a cup of coffee that smelled a wee bit like whiskey.

There hadn't been any judgment or fear. Just complete love and support that if he stopped and thought about it now, it might just have him crying like a babe.

But what he remembered feeling that night was just embarrassment and anger that Vivian had done this to him. Yeah, yeah. He'd done it to himself.

The fact that, after they'd waited for years, she'd slept with a guy as soon as they'd broken up...

But telling his parents he was still a virgin ranked up there right after telling the principal he'd been involved in attempting to steal the mascot from their rivals... and had nearly gotten his ear bitten off by the darn goat.

They'd been supportive and said about a million times that no matter what he did, he'd always have a home with them.

That's when they told him Vivian's mom was going to kick her out. They had anticipated moving her in with them since it was their grandbaby, but now they asked him what he wanted to do.

Man, he'd been an idiot. His first thought was that this was her problem. He'd been mad and just generally pissed off at his (very good) world at that point. After letting him rage for a few moments, his dad looked him in the eye and said something that changed everything.

"Son, I can see how hurt you are, but do you love the girl or not?"

And everything flipped. Just, bam, right in that moment.

In his mind, a picture he'd never thought to consider formed. Of him and Vivian sitting where his parents were sitting when they were old—Omgosh, in their forties!—and everything being... right.

"Yes," was all he said.

"Then she can come here." His mom gave his dad a nod and he went on. "There will be rules."

"Lots of rules."

And Cam knew he'd agree to every one of them to keep her safe.

But it had been too late. Vivian was already gone. Driven to the train down the coast and off to an unknown aunt somewhere far, far away.

He was remembering it all, feeling every emotion again, as he waded through his sketchbooks, looking at the best and most varied work he'd done of the sleigh, finding some old pictures he'd forgotten and trying to put the day Vivian left behind him—again—when his mother called up.

"Dinner in five."

7

VIVIAN

VIVIAN WAS NOT happy to be heading home without the sleigh. Apparently there were some swanky insurance guys coming and she couldn't touch it until they'd done a full review of the damage.

She pulled up her schedule and tried to sort through what was what. She was in a dire situation, but all she could hear over and over again was Camden Ross telling her he loved her and always had.

And Lyra doubling down on it.

It was not the distraction she needed.

Sure, he'd been her first love—and as first loves went, he was a great one. That was why he was stuck on this. On her.

It wasn't like women weren't basically falling at his feet on a regular basis. It was almost ridiculous to watch them when he, Noah, and Jamie went to The Lighthouse, the local pub.

She forced her mind back to work. And then forced it back again.

When she'd returned to Starlight Harbor, she'd had to struggle to get jobs. Not just because she was a woman, but because small towns had long memories. Now she was afraid if she handed off any of that work to the garage just outside town, she'd never earn it back again.

She pulled her hair out of the bun it was in and ran a French braid down the back of her head, needing to do something with her hands as she thought about her options.

None of them were good.

She was running at capacity which, of course, was a huge blessing. With a nine-year-old boy just starting another growth spurt, she knew she'd be needing one more round of summer clothes and then all new school clothes over the next couple months.

And the food. My goodness, the food.

Did all kids eat like this?

It was going to take some really long days. She might have to find a babysitter for Tyler. There was no way she could be a present mom for the next sixteen days.

If she thought he'd be safe with Ms. Angie, she'd be packing his bag and dropping him off on her porch. But she kind of wanted to keep her son safe, sane, and out of jail, so that was a no go.

Of course, Tyler wasn't the only issue as she circled back to Cam.

She still had to figure out what to do about him. They were going to be stuck in close quarters together for the next two weeks. And there wasn't really a lot of room around that. He'd have to be over here working on the sleigh when she was doing her other jobs. It wasn't like she could move it over to his place when it was his turn to work on it.

Maybe she could put Tyler and Cam on a fishing boat and send them off for a month of hard labor. Then she could have some peace for a couple days.

Another hour later and her focus had narrowed to just

the sleigh and making it go again. Preferably without dying or blowing up in the middle of the parade.

She had a surprising amount of research to do after a glance at the dinosaur of an engine. And they were losing time every moment the insurance company kept doing their thing.

"Mom! Can we order pizza?" Tyler shouted down the stairs to the garage.

The fact she was exhausted, filthy, and nowhere near done for the night made her shout back, "Yes. Call Jonah and ask him to deliver."

"Soda?" a hopeful shout came back.

"Nope. You lost any chance at soda this afternoon."

There was a long pause while she waited for an argument or a retreat. When the door finally closed, she got back to work. She had some time to research before the sleigh was brought over.

She was contemplating if just replacing the entire engine was a better way to go. The hardware under the hood was amazingly old and had been cared for in a daily-maintenance type of way—not the ongoing care that would be needed to keep a classic going for a long life.

Which, in Starlight Harbor, was forever.

This might be the best chance to handle that since any issues created could be watched over and cared for by Cam as they went.

She pulled up a parts site to see if she could find something she could work with in one of the local junkyards. Everything she was finding was little sports cars. She wanted something that would run forever and could deal with the sleigh's weight.

An old Miata did not fit the bill.

She just put out three texts to guys in the area telling them what she needed when she saw Cam's dad pull into the lot, Cam chatting away in the front seat, his typically happy self. The two of them laughed together before Cam hopped out and circled the car to where the trunk had been popped. He pulled out a few boxes, stacking them one on top of the other before heading toward his place.

Leave it to Cam to still be moving out of his parents' house five years after moving in over here.

His mother was probably boxing up his room little by little and sending him home with something every week.

The knock on the side door pulled her out of her thoughts about figuring out how to remove the wood-deco-rated hood so she could get a safe space around the engine for the replacement.

She hit the intercom that was attached to the apart-ment. "Tyler, run down and grab the pizza. I'll be up in a minute."

"'Kay!"

She was not looking forward to the fact that on top of everything going on, she still had to do mom-duty tonight after Tyler's lying and safety situation.

Counting to ten wasn't going to help with the frame of mind she was already in.

And the fact she was even considering letting him work with Cam was giving her a headache.

Heading upstairs, she was happily surprised to see pizza, plates, and napkins all on the table like quasi-civilized humans.

While she might have momentarily forgotten the upcoming conversation, obviously Tyler hadn't.

That at least was a good sign.

She washed up and headed in to find Tyler sitting at the table with his book.

"Finish the page, then it's dinnertime." She grabbed the pitcher of iced tea from the kitchen and headed back to where Tyler had put his book aside faster than ever and with absolutely no arguing.

Yeah, her son was no fool.

Neither was she—she'd let him sweat it for a bit.

"What do you think about the sleigh?" she asked instead.

And was shocked at exactly how many thoughts her son had on the topic. From the history of the work to the artist to the things he bet Cam would have to do to try to repair it.

Of course, in Tyler's view, it was a done deal since Cam was the Hero of Everything in her son's eyes.

She was just about to segue into the "you're one step away from grounded for the rest of your life and if you ever lie to me again" talk when there was a knock at the door.

Tyler all but leapt out of his seat, obviously sensing the change in focus rolling off his mom.

"Mom! Cam's here!"

Of course, because that's what she needed right now.

"Saved by the bell," she mumbled under her breath, not knowing if she was referring to herself or Tyler.

"Hey." Cam stepped into the dining room, a grin on his face. "I hate to disturb your dinner, but we've been summoned by the High Council of the Harbor."

"We have a high council?" Tyler asked, bouncing on his feet as if a quest was the next thing on the docket.

"No, honey. Cam is making a joke. We have selectmen."

"They're all men?"

"Well, no. Sometimes they're women, but the word has stuck from when it was all men."

Tyler thought about that for a minute, something she'd learned a long time ago to respect. She had no idea where her son's patience to stop and consider things came from, but she'd rather that than her impetuous, rush-into-stupidity gene she'd worked hard to squash for over a decade.

"That's stupid," was what he finally came up with.

"That's my boy." She gave him a wide grin. "So, the summon?"

"Yeah, town council meeting tonight to discuss the sleigh fiasco."

"Great, just what we need. All the chefs and their understudies in the kitchen."

"I think they also want to do some Captain Jack shaming."

"You mean Ms. Angie shaming."

"You know, if it were possible to shame that woman, I'd be all for it." Cam flashed her a grin. "But I'm pretty sure nothing short of walking naked through the parade would do it."

"Mom, you should bring a sign."

She glanced at Tyler. "Why's that, hon?"

"Because they do that on the internet. Dog shaming. Like they take a picture of him looking sad that says *I ate Mom's favorite shoes*. And then he won't do it anymore."

The adults shared a glance, both wondering if there was any reason to discuss the whole dogs-can't-read thing right now. Vivian shook her head with a laugh and figured, what the heck?

"A dog drove a sleigh today, so why not?"

Sign shaming it was.

"Sure." Cam flashed Tyler a grin. "You got a sign on you, buddy?"

Tyler's eyes narrowed and Vivian saw one of the few

things that reminded her of Ty's dad. He used to get that very determined look before a game back in high school.

"I could make one."

"Okay, why don't you go grab your sign-making stuff."

She watched as Tyler rushed out of the room on his mission, pretty sure that wasn't just a casual move on Cam's part.

"So..." She walked her plate to the sink. "How much time do I have?" she asked before Cam could get side-tracked like he had this morning with his weird deals and surprise I love yous.

Cam glanced at his watch and *she* got distracted by his forearms. The man had lean, strong arms. The kind that weren't obvious, but stretched out with such grace when he was working with the machines in his studio that any woman would stop to drool—er, stare at.

He was, to her way of thinking, built just right.

Which was one more reason she tried to stay away from him as much as possible. She wasn't looking for a man, no matter how he was put together.

"Just enough time for you to get everything you need, for someone to make a sign, and for me to pop some popcorn."

"Do you really think that's the best idea?"

"I've had better for sure. But I've absolutely also had worse. And honestly, these meetings are better than going over to the drive-in. You hustle up and get your stuff together. I'll take care of the snacks."

"Yeah, the snacks in my cupboard." She didn't fight too hard since there was no way Tyler would make it through the meeting without a complaint or two of being starved to death. She left it at that and went to change into more appropriate leave-the-house clothing.

She also needed to make sure they were on the same page *at least* in a professional capacity. No need to walk into the lion's den unprepared, she thought as she changed.

And completely tried to ignore the fact that Cam Ross was in her kitchen making himself right at home.

8

CAM

CAM WASN'T GOING to lie.

He got a huge kick out of these town meetings. There was something about the drama of it all that just made him grin like a maniac.

Of course, he usually didn't have a dog in the fight, so he could sit back and watch the local factions throw down over everything from how to hide recycling for aesthetics to if having fresh Christmas trees year-round was acceptable.

He wasn't really sure what this meeting would entail since the plan of action—him dealing with the external, Vivian dealing with the internal—was already decided. Of course, that was an on-the-spot declaration by Ms. Angie.

But the decision made sense to him. He and Vivian were the best people in town for the job. And not to brag, but he was one of the best. Period. He was already making sure he lowered his fee behind closed doors so they didn't have to challenge Vivian's pay.

And even if they did want to fly in experts, he was the expert they'd most likely have flown in. There were few people who had studied Raymond Havester as in depth as he had, had the woodworking experience and awards, and would actually be able to handle both the historical and hands-on aspect of the job.

And if they did try to underpay Vivian? Well, he'd have strong language in reserve.

While Tyler had finished eating, sign-making, and cleaning up, he and Vivian created a plan of attack.

Okay, more of a plan of "sit back and let them hack it to shreds, then step in and tell them as directly as possible what they needed to make this happen."

Watching Vivian attempt to sit back and keep her mouth shut was going to be amusing.

When Vivian finally came downstairs in a jean skirt and a fitted t-shirt, he gave her a grin. This was a different type of armor than she usually wore and he was fascinated by the change.

And proud of her. She wasn't trying to sell them her abilities now—she had to know she'd proven her talent with cars over and over again. Now she was dressed for town business.

Man, he loved this woman.

It took everything in him not to reach over and take her hand as they climbed the hill to town hall, waving to the parade of people heading up around them and listening to the small talk.

They were one of the last groups into the hall, even if almost no one had taken their seats yet. And by a stroke of luck or planning, there were a couple seats in a middle row they were waved to.

Cam motioned for Tyler to go first and let his hand fall to Vivian's waist as they wound their way through the crowd of gossiping people who couldn't seem to figure out if this was exciting or a tragedy.

Vivian kept shifting under his touch. Tough luck, toots. She was going to have to let him woo her, including all the old-school gentleman moves he could pull out of his hat.

Maybe his dad would have some good old-timey suggestions.

Flowers seemed trite for a woman as vivid as Vivian.

Maybe new wrenches?

She probably had too many of those already.

When they got to the empty seats, Vivian shrugged his hand off and stepped into the row first, seating Tyler between them.

Cam flashed her a smile. That was fine. He loved Tyler, too.

Cam froze, realizing the thought that had just slipped through his mind with such ease that if he'd been more distracted, he wouldn't have noticed it.

He loved Tyler, too.

The stakes got higher every time he let his brain do the thinking.

Something must have shown on his face because as he glanced around, his gaze clashed with his mom's across the aisle and a few rows back looking smugly pleased to see him with Vivian and Ty until she caught his eye.

"Are you okay?" she mouthed, causing him to wipe his face clear of all expression.

Now wasn't the time.

He flashed her a reassuring smile and turned to face forward as Selectperson McCreary pounded her gavel with surprising strength for her age.

Let the show begin.

9

———

VIVIAN

THIS WAS NOT GOING the way Vivian had expected it to.

There were calls for an investigation. Shouts of culture ruined. Suggestions that perhaps it was time to just do away with the sleigh—the last one was met with outright horror from most of the crowd.

She'd expected the typical shenanigans, but once Jonathan Baines stepped on the stage, she felt herself—and most of the room—let out a deep groan.

He looked to Selectperson McCreary as if he expected a big introduction, but she just rolled her eyes and grumbled, "Jonathan, we all know who you are."

"Well." He glanced around as if this couldn't be true in their town of 348 people. "*As you know*, I'm Jonathan Baines, Town Financial Officer—"

"Accountant," the selectperson interjected to a room full of snickers.

"And as such," he continued as if no one had spoken, "I've done some research on the cost of repairing the sled and bringing in the right people to do it."

Cam growled under his breath and Vi wasn't surprised to see the entire town turn to look at him.

"That was fast," a muted complaint came from a few rows back.

"I've already gathered a list of acceptable candidates available through a program I partner with for the Maine Cultural Society." The accountant seemed far more smug than pleased. Vivian wasn't sure she liked where this was going. "I've certified their résumés and they can come up as soon as we complete the call for interest on the project."

Before he even finished speaking, Cam was on his feet.

"You? You've decided who's qualified to work on our local art?" Cam crossed his arms, sticking his hands under his armpits. Vivian could see they were balled into tight fists.

"I'm sorry, Camden," Jonathan countered with a sneer. "Was there something that makes you think you're more qualified than I am? Only one of us has a degree from Harvard."

If Cam was ever going to punch someone, she was pretty sure it was right now.

She glanced to the front of the room where Skye stood in her deputy's outfit, arms crossed, looking resigned to arresting one of her best friends.

But she also wasn't stepping in, so Vi was betting Cam would get at least one swing in.

Skye was fair like that.

"I don't know, *accountant*." Cam put as much warmth into the statement as Jonathan had. "Could it be my years of studying the artist, or the fact that I had an internship with his estate's studio before I was even out of high school? Or maybe the three years running that Maine called me the

premier wood artist of my generation... I mean *our* generation? You're the premier what?"

From across the aisle, Vivian was pretty sure she heard
Jamie snort and mumble, "Premier jackass."

Around him, a couple people snickered, so she upped
that to pretty *darn* sure.

"I"—Jonathan put way more emphasis on that pronoun
than any normal person would—"am the person making the
decisions here."

Behind him, Selectperson McCreary dropped her head
into her hands. She probably figured she'd let this play out,
let Jonathan make a bigger ass of himself, then figure out
how to move forward—hopefully without Cam wrecking
one of the hands he needed to complete the job.

Or maybe Vivian was just projecting.

"Absolutely not." Camden was practically vibrating
next to her. "We're not letting some hack who knows
nothing about art or culture, and shockingly little about our
town's history, make decisions that will impact a living piece
of antiquity that's vital to our town and basically a historical
touchstone for the entire state."

There was a smattering of applause from the far side of
the room as three old men stamped their canes on the floor.

Geez, the lairds were here. This had the potential to get
really ugly.

"I don't know what makes you think you deserve that
right." Jonathan had his arms crossed, an officious stance
that did nothing to break Jamie's accusation about his
premier spot in the town.

The audience's gaze was jumping between the two
men, like a small tennis match they were stuck in the
middle of.

"Jonathan, if you're still looking for something to measure against me, maybe art knowledge shouldn't be it." Cam rolled his eyes and shook his head.

The fact was, there wasn't anyone in town who could measure their knowledge of art against Cam. In fact, there were very few in Maine who could measure their knowledge about Raymond Havester against him.

"Believe it or not, Cam, this has nothing to do with you. Not everything is about you."

Chairs squeaked as everyone turned forward to watch Jonathan, then back to get Cam's reaction.

"Mom," a little voice came in her ear. "Who is this guy?"

Oh, geez.

"Do you have a guy that's mean to you and you can't figure out why?"

"Yes, Mikey Baines."

Great, runs in the family.

"That was the guy for Cam. And Cam could have taken him down but was always the bigger man."

"That's why Uncle Jamie doesn't like him."

"That and seven thousand other reasons."

"Got it." He sat back, way more invested in this than she expected.

Of course his hero was front and center, so... yeah.

"I have no interest in everything in this town being about me. That sounds like the most exhausting thing since, well, dealing with you. Absolutely anytime I've had to deal with you was more than enough town-centric time for me."

"Go Uncle Cam!" Tyler's little voice carried across the room to a huff of muffled laughter.

Cam turned, his whole body loosening up. "Thanks, bud."

"Okay"—Vivian leaned down—"that was your one involvement moment, got it?"

Tyler nodded, looking particularly pleased with himself.

Jonathan shot a glare at Tyler and Vivian nearly came out of her chair.

"Well, I am—" Jonathan glanced down as this phone dinged several times in a row. He lifted it to read the screen, a rush of red going up his cheeks. "My client says they would be more than willing to let you review the applications. Although I have already chosen the people who will be assisting on this job."

Before Jonathan could lower the phone, it dinged again.

He glanced at it, his eyebrows coming down in an obvious effort not to frown. "Although, my client states that your input is valuable, and if we have any issues, they would like to hear about them ahead of time."

Obviously, this was not the power move Jonathan had been hoping to make. It felt very much like, "Well, Mom said I have to let you play with my ball."

The ball being a nearly century-old piece of Americana.

The ding chimed again.

Vivian snorted, while people watched as Jonathan tried to pretend nothing weird had just happened.

Finally, someone on the other side of the room shouted, "Well? What does it say?"

"This one was personal," Jonathan replied primly and stuck his cell in his pocket.

Jamie snorted loud enough for everyone to hear this time and stated, "It probably told him to stop being a jackass."

The entire meeting cracked up while Selectperson McCreary banged the gavel.

"That's enough." She banged it again, starting to look frustrated that everyone wasn't settling down. "I said that's enough. We obviously have the beginnings of a solution. Camden Ross and Vivian Breck will be paid for their services, additional help will be brought in, and Jonathan will stop being a jackass."

Vivian laid her head in her hands and tried not to laugh at what she wouldn't approve of her son saying.

From farther back in the room, someone who sounded suspiciously like Camden's mother added, "Good luck with that."

Before anyone could add to the chaos of the meeting, the selectperson called for adjournment and hurried out the back door, leaving anyone who might question her behind.

"What about Captain Jack?" Tyler asked. "I didn't get to use my sign."

Vivian only managed not to snort because she loved her son. "I am one hundred percent sure you will get to use your sign sometime in the not-too-distant future the way Captain Jack is out there breaking all the laws."

He seemed content with the idea that at some point he'd get to dog shame the captain and tucked his stuff away in his backpack.

Everyone rose, knowing there wasn't going to be any more decision-making tonight—at least not formally.

But that didn't mean anything in Starlight Harbor. Only people like Jonathan and to some extent the selectmen believed that. Most people knew the truth though.

Because of that, there was a slow exit while everyone glanced to the far left-hand side of the room where the three older gentlemen sat, heads together.

Vivian would give up her best pro-lift to know what they were saying.

When the collective waved Noah over, she suspected she wouldn't have to wait too long.

10

CAM

CAMDEN WAS 99.8% sure his head was going to explode.

Of course, Jonathan Baines had to stick his nose in where it didn't belong. He'd been looking for a way to be the hero. If he wasn't so much of a—in Jamie's (and maybe his mother's) words—jackass, Cam might've felt bad for him at some point.

Some very, very distant point.

But Jonathan had always used Cam and Jamie, and their friend Rob Dunn until he moved away, as the stepping stool to build himself up.

He'd always seemed a little desperate.

The only time Cam had ever hit someone was when Jonathan started the rumor Cam admitted to being then-pregnant Vivian's baby daddy and he had coldheartedly told her she was on her own.

Of course, it'd been Jonathan's brother who had gotten Vivian pregnant and disappeared.

Cam wasn't sure which reason was a better one: trying

to ruin his reputation as a teenager or trying to destroy the town's legacy just to get a one-up.

Of course, adult Cam could see the rumors also deeply hurt Vivian, so in retrospect it was a no-brainer. But Jonathan had done so many things to tick Cam off for decades that each one felt like the worst at the time.

But now he'd gone too far.

About six miles too far.

"Hey." Vivian rested a hand on his arm where it was crossed in an attempt to keep it under control. "Don't worry. No one is going to let Jonathan take over and ruin it. It's one thing for him to pretend he came up with the money himself, it's completely another for him to actually be able to do the work. We all know he and his stupid spreadsheets wouldn't know the difference between a cedar bowl and Tupperware."

Cam felt some of the tension ease out of him. Vivian was right. This wasn't a battle he was going to have to fight alone. Already, his parents were weaving their way through the crowd, smiling and nodding in a way that said they didn't want to be rude but they had somewhere to be.

Probably over here making sure Cam didn't punch Jonathan for the second time in his life.

He glanced up at Vivian who was watching him with an odd but fierce expression on her face.

He forced an easygoing grin and winked at her.

"Hey." Vivian nudged him and nodded her head toward where the lairds sat. "What do you think that's all about?"

On the far side of the room, Noah bent at the waist to listen to the older men, rubbing at the back of his neck like he was trying to get rid of a few layers of skin.

"No idea, but hopefully we'll have a clue soon."

Which meant meeting at Noah's.

"Camden!" His mother waved her hand high in the air as if at six-two he wouldn't be able to see her over a crowd. She and his father worked their way down the aisle, excusing themselves as people mulled around grumbling about the lack of real action and a lot of things about *outsiders* being discussed.

Cam felt a little surge of pride.

The town seemed to trust him.

No matter how many times Jonathan tried to destroy his reputation.

"I have never liked that—" She stopped short when Tyler's head popped out from behind Vivian and pivoted, finishing with, "Jerk. Why every time you have any type of issue, he's behind it. Since you were this one's age. It got old two decades ago. I should have a word with his mother."

Cam snorted. Leave it to his mom to try to mom-solve.

Man, he loved his parents.

She waved at Tyler and he smiled up at her shyly.

"It's gonna be what it's gonna be," Cam said, trying to stay outwardly even-toned.

He wasn't dumb. His mother could start a riot with her pinky finger.

A good portion of the room—including Jonathan himself—had had Mrs. Ross for English and still loved her.

Not that he wasn't tempted to let her.

"But something's going on." Vivian pointed again over to the lairds and Mrs. Ross smirked.

"That should have been my first stop. What do they want with Noah?"

"No idea." Cam had known the old men had been hanging out more and more in Noah's café, but he figured it was because the pub had started getting too rowdy for them. Probably a stupid assumption. They probably started half the brawls that happened in the building. "But we'll head over to Noah's and find out."

His mother gave a nod as Vivian shook her head.

"Sorry, no babysitter and I have a feeling Noah's will have drinking and adult language." She gave a little grin as she said it and he wondered how many small things she missed out on to be the supermom she was.

"That's no problem." His mother reached out and patted Vivian's arm. "Harry and I can take him. If you don't mind that is. Harry's working on a new puzzle and could use a willing victim. Would Tyler be interested? I'd pay him in cookies."

"Hey, now. Those are my cookies." Cam wrapped an arm around her shoulder and gave a little squeeze.

"You snooze, you lose, Camden." She turned back to Vivian and looked less sure. "That is, if Vivian is comfortable with him coming over. If you think it's going to be late, he could stay. Or we could bring him back. Or you could come get him..."

His mother faded out and it was then he realized she was a little unsure about the outcome of the suggestion.

11

VIVIAN

VIVIAN HAD to pause for a second, thinking it over. It wasn't like she and Tyler had never been apart. He went to school. He went to camp. He had a babysitter—or as he stated, the person who hung out with him while Mom was busy. But there was something next-level about him going over to the Rosses'.

She looked at Mrs. Ross's face which was filled with an odd kind of hope, and Vi couldn't deal with the idea of saying no to her.

And honestly, would there really be any better place for Tyler to be than their house?

"Sure," she said. "I'll warn you though, he's a handful."

"Oh, please." Mrs. Ross waved a hand between them. "You've met my sons. A handful is an understatement."

Beside her, Tyler watched the entire exchange carefully. Vivian had to remember this was a first for him as well.

Mrs. Ross's child-radar must have pinged on. "If you'll give me a sec, I have to have a word with Jenny. Then I'll be right back and we can get this show on the road."

She waited until Mrs. Ross was several feet away before turning back to Tyler. "You're okay with this while I go figure out what's going on? It's this or go to another meeting."

Even though she knew she was not making him go sit through Noah's. He was getting that tired look around the eyes that never boded well for cooperation.

Heck, she was probably getting it too if she was being honest.

"Yeah. Cam's parents are cool. I mean they come down and help out at camp sometimes."

"They do?"

"Yeah," Tyler said again, waving at a friend just past her right shoulder.

"Ty?"

"Oh, yeah. Mr. Ross is my batting coach. He said I have a lot of potential. Cam says they used to watch videos to make him better when he was in high school." His attention drifted away for another moment and Vivian waved a hand. "Do you think Mr. Ross would watch batting videos with me?"

"There's not much he'd love more." Cam stepped back up to them. "He loves coaching. He'd still be doing it if he hadn't—gotten sick a few years ago."

Mr. Ross had had a straight-up heart attack in his forties, but she appreciated Cam dodging that info.

"Wow, like one-on-one coaching. And Mikey Baines not there to push his nose in."

Not a selling point Vivian had anticipated, but sure.

"But remember, they worked all day. If they're not up for a video, then maybe just watch a movie or something."

"PG-13?"

"Yeah, we'll leave that call up to Mr. and Mrs. Ross. I'm sure they have some options we'd all be happy with."

Cam gave a barely there head bob and Mrs. Ross made her way back over.

"Ms. Bev! I'm going to come over and hang out with you guys. Cam said maybe we can watch some batting videos."

Mrs. Ross gave a deep sigh. "I guess you'll be too busy to help me bake some cookies, then."

"Oh, cookies." Tyler sounded so torn that Cam had to turn a snort into a cough.

"With all your mom is going to have to do over the next little bit, I'm betting we'll get to have you come visit again. If not, we can make a baking date for just the two of us later."

Vivian was in awe of the woman.

Mrs. Ross looked up at her and smiled. "Don't worry. We'll have a great time."

Before she knew what was happening, Tyler was bee boppin' his way down the aisle with a last look back when he reached the end and shouted, "Bye, Mom!"

Cam wrapped an arm around her shoulder and leaned in. "My mother is going to be in heaven. She misses having younger kids around even if she loves teaching high school."

"Do they do the grandkids-pressure thing?"

Cam shrugged. "Not really. But I think it's because they get the whole finding-the-right-person thing." He looked down and smiled at her like he was biting his tongue.

As soon as she saw that look, she realized he was starting to make some moves and eased out from under his arm.

"Cam—"

"Hey, none of that. We've got to get over to Noah's."

With that, he turned and followed Tyler down their aisle.

She grabbed all their stuff since neither of them thought of picking up their trash and glanced around the room.

On the far side, Noah still stood in front of the lairds, shaking his head like he was ready to escape the madness.

When one of them put both hands on his turned-oak cane she'd place darn good money Cam had made for him and moved to rise, Noah stepped forward. Even obviously frustrated, he was going to be polite and show respect to his elders.

Of course, Vivian couldn't hold back the snort she let loose when the man took a swipe at Noah's hand and swatted it away.

Noah gave one last shake of his head and stalked off.

Well, this should be interesting.

She spotted Skye at the front of the room, braced at the foot of the stairs that led to the stage. She was taking no prisoners and seemed ready for anything—so, basically on-brand Skye.

Below her station, Lyra spoke with a woman who seemed bent on sharing her opinion of the evening with someone. As always, Lyra was the safe space people needed. But as they'd found out just this past month, she had more of a steel spine than any of them had suspected.

Especially when it came to Starlight Harbor.

And, unfortunately, everything tonight had to do with it, so Lyra was probably ready to rumble.

Oh, no!

Vivian stutter-stepped to a stop. Did that mean... was *she* the one left to be the voice of reason tonight?

"Hey." Jamie stepped up next to her, watching Lyra and Skye subtly maneuver the woman back toward the crowd and for a moment Vivian thought, *Jamie!* with relief.

But then, of course, she thought, *Oh. Jamie. No.*

"We're heading over to Noah's to see what all the proclamations going down with the lairds were."

"Saw that," Jamie answered, still scanning the room. "Even as I was watching to make sure I didn't have to break up a fight."

"Please, break up?"

"It would give me an excuse to get a swing in." Jamie grinned, completely unrepentant. "That guy has been harassing Cam for as long as I can remember. No idea why."

He paused in a way that said what everyone thought: Maybe because of her.

But it had started way before she was out of pigtails. Not that she and Cam hadn't been throwing each other glances on the playground too.

"Is it because he's more talented, a better athlete, smarter, better-looking, and basically the town sweetheart?"

"Huh, and here I thought Lyra was the town sweetheart. Can dudes be the sweetheart?"

Vivian could already see the wheels turning. She would lay good money on there being a Mr. Starlight Contest in the not-so-distant future.

"Anyway," she rushed on before he could start plotting. "I'm grabbing the girls and we're heading over to Noah's."

"Where's mini-you?"

"With the Rosses."

Jamie opened his mouth, then—showing more wisdom than he usually did—he snapped it shut again.

"Smart move," Vivian said as she walked away.

"I'll just, you know, grab Cam... meet you there..."

She was still shaking her head when she finally made it to Lyra.

"What's up?"

"We're meeting at Noah's."

At the words, Lyra grinned a little. Her boyfriend, Spence, had recently moved in with Noah. Even though he was away for the weekend, she still seemed to get that little spark from heading to his space.

"Hey, I've got some day-afters at the store no one bought. Probably because they were all stalking the drama. Let's swing by and grab them."

"Speaking my love language right there." Vivian turned to look at Skye on the second step to the stage, surveying her battlefield. "We're going to the bakery, then to Noah's to regroup. You in?"

Skye glanced down, her gray eyes always calm in cop-situations. "If these people will leave and go home peace-fully, I'll be right over."

Honestly, if the government knew about Skye, there'd be world peace with her in charge.

Her sheriff knew he had gold in a uniform with her, even as her very literal brain sometimes created situations he had to—well, smooth over.

Vivian rejoined Lyra who was already waiting at the side door everyone was ignoring so they could bump into each other and gossip at the double oak doors, then the wide granite stairs outside, then the spacious grassy area that led down to the backside of the town square.

Which was absolutely too many places for someone to stop them to talk.

"This..." Lyra grinned as they walked down the old path that led past what was once the school—yes, the entire school. "This is perfect. It gives me a chance to ask about all those glances Cam was throwing your way and all your not-so-subtle attempts to dodge said glances."

She could lie.

Lyra wouldn't let her get away with it, but she could totally lie.

Then they'd do the dance. And Lyra would pull the friend card and start being the new non-pushover version of herself.

"We got in a fight and he said he still loves me." That should cover it.

Lyra tripped over an invisible crack in the sidewalk and nearly took a header before Vi grabbed her arm.

"Wow." She looked up at Vivian, eyes wide. "I guess I didn't expect you to just spit it out. You two have absolutely no romantic subtlety between the two of you."

Vivian rolled her eyes, afraid she'd just opened up a place for Lecture Lyra to step into.

"Which," Lyra went on before Vi could divert her, "is exactly why you're perfect for each other."

Vivian should have seen it coming when they'd walked over to the meeting together. She'd definitely figured his parents would side-eye them when he'd been all *Mr. You Walk Ahead and I'll Just Rest My Hand Here On Your Back.*

But it was her own fault for missing Lyra.

She was sneaky.

People needed to stop underestimating her.

Lyra, that was. Vivian didn't expect people to ever stop underestimating her.

She glanced down as she shortened her steps to match Lyra's, only to catch her texting.

"Um, whatcha doing?"

"Nothing."

Yeah, right. She took her elbow and steered her around the raised block Lyra tripped over when she *was* paying attention.

"Try again."

"Okay, just, you know, texting Spence."

She sounded way too innocent.

"About me and Cam." It wasn't a question.

"Spence called it his first weekend here. And everyone likes to be encouraged when they're right." She lowered her phone and smiled. "He's going to love having been right. Noah said Cam wasn't that much of a masochist."

"Hey!"

"Not that you're not great, but honestly—you put out some pretty clear vibes that you're not available." Her phone dinged and she lifted it as she turned the screen back on. "*Especially* about Cam. And Spence didn't even know your history."

Vivian noted the "didn't even" was past tense.

"Anyway," Lyra continued as if Vivian wasn't going to push her into the shrubbery, "Spence thinks you guys are perfect for each other. He says that outsiders sometimes see things the most clearly."

"Isn't this the guy you had a war with because he called Starlight Harbor tacky?"

"That," Lyra sniffed, "was before he saw it. Then he outsider-loved it."

12

CAM

CAM CARRIED a tray with glasses and a pitcher of iced tea out to Noah's deck, grinning at the very homeyness of it.

"Not a word. You'd be walking back and forth to get all this stuff and Skye gave it to me because she wanted to be helpful."

Of course he wouldn't say anything in front of Skye. She sometimes didn't know when you were teasing her and when you weren't, and they all loved her enough to only tease in ways that would absolutely not hurt her feelings.

"Dude, if it were just the little tray, that would be one thing. But I swear you've been hanging out with my mom for cozy cottage lessons."

"If your mom taught that, the class would be packed, so I'd think twice about mentioning it in front of her."

The man was not wrong.

Ding.

They all looked to where Spence leaned happily against the railing, typing away on his cell.

At the silence, he glanced up.

"So." Spence smirked. "You thought in the middle of an

BACK TO YOU   71

argument was the best time to tell Vivian you're still in love with her? Even I wasn't that stupid."

As one, the guys turned to him with matching looks of disbelief on their faces. And then Jamie lost it.

"Oh, wow. This is literally the best thing that has happened since Lyra threatened Spence's life and caused a traffic jam on the square."

"Two cars is not a traffic jam." Spence crossed his arms. "And one of them was Ms. Angie who was just there to escalate the situation as much as possible."

Out of the corner of his eye, Cam saw Jamie nudge Noah and both men settled back into their seats as if pulling up a great movie they'd seen a few times already.

Cam ran a hand through his hair and figured, what the hell?

"Yup. We were having a fight about Tyler learning woodworking and she turned that into *our past*." He put air quotes around it in case his annoyed tone wasn't enough of a key indicator. "So I figured, she opened the door, let's put it all out there and... yeah, I might have shouted at her that I still loved her."

The guys glanced at one another before simultaneously breaking into laughter.

"Oh, man." Noah had to take a deep breath and then waved his hand to keep going because apparently he had more laughing to do.

"Yeah, she took me about as seriously as you guys." Cam reached out and poured himself more tea, putting the pitcher firmly down on the table with a look when Jamie held his glass out for a refill. "And I want to absolutely thank you for your support."

Noah shook his head, almost done laughing.

"Okay, first off, I support you and Vivian. I mean, this

situation right here is a perfect example. I don't know another woman you could yell at that you love them and still have a chance."

"Amen," Jamie added, as he reached for the pitcher and gave Cam an aggrieved glare.

"But I'm not sure bringing Tyler into this was your best move."

"I didn't bring him into it. It started with him." Cam gave a quick rundown of the afternoon, all the work he'd been doing with Tyler when Vivian had shown up, and the fight that ensued.

They nodded along, none of them surprised and all of them secretly happy Cam was finally getting his rear in gear to win her back.

"I mean, I thought this would be way easier." He stretched out his legs, trying to shake off all the day's blows. "I figured, well, look at Spence."

Jamie and Noah nodded their agreement.

"Wait, what does that mean? Look at Spence?"

And Spence has entered the conversation.

The troublemaker should be so happy he was just now being brought up since he's the one who started it with the texts from Lyra.

"You basically showed up as Lyra's archnemesis. If you can make a comeback from that, I should be able to recover from a stupid situation when I was sixteen. Who hasn't done something completely idiotic when they were that age?"

"Me," Spence said with absolute surety.

"Okay, so you missed sixteen, but you managed to hit some mistakes out of the park after that if I recall."

Spence saluted him with his iced tea. "True. Very true."

"So," Jamie jumped back in, "how are you going to win her back?"

"Obviously I'm going to woo her."

There was a weighted moment of silence before the men burst out laughing again.

"Vivian?"

"Yes, Vivian. If I want to marry Vivian, why would I woo someone else?"

Jamie snorted. "That might actually be easier. Vivian isn't exactly... wooable?"

"What Jamie is trying to say," Noah stepped in, "is that Vivian is less traditional than Lyra and that wooing might look a little different."

"Yeah. No kidding. I mean, she's very practical. And straightforward. She likes things that make her home feel clutter-free but homey. And her business is incredibly important to her—not just its success, but its reputation. She wants to be respected and doesn't believe she is. Tyler obviously needs to be the center of her world. I'm not sure if she even likes flowers and stuff."

"All women like flowers and stuff. You just need to find out what the flowers and stuff are that they like."

They all turned toward Spence. "Like, Lyra loves her bakery but doesn't eat a lot of sweets, right? They all have their own *and stuff*. But no matter what, the respect thing— that's spot-on."

"Okay, you're not a complete idiot about this," Cam conceded.

"You know—" Before Jamie could throw whatever the crazy idea he was probably forming into the fray, they heard the front door fall shut.

"Hello! We're here!" Lyra wandered out, hands full of a

basket with little bags of cookies and sweets. Her gaze immediately slid to Spence. "Oh my gosh! You're here!"

She tossed the cookies at the table and threw herself into his arms.

"You said you'd be back tomorrow. You said that like ten minutes ago, you big liar!"

Spence swept her into his arms and kissed her in a way that had them all glancing away for a second. "I missed you too much. Driving extra today didn't seem like a big deal."

They stood there grinning at each other like fools until Vivian brushed past them.

"We can open these cookies, right? Because it looks like people somehow overlooked the cinnamon spice ones this week."

Spence pulled out a chair for Lyra and put a glass of tea in front of her before settling himself down as close as the arms of their chairs would allow.

Cam, feeling like he was already behind the ball, jumped up and pulled out the chair next to him, waving a hand between it and Vivian.

"Can I get you something to drink?" he asked.

Vivian just looked at him like he was nuts. "Am I going to have to tip you at the end of the night if you do?"

Cam opened his mouth, but before he could respond, Noah interjected, "Don't. Just don't."

"Um, no. No tip necessary."

Vivian sat in the chair, glancing around the table with a look of frustrated impatience.

"Yes, Cam told me he loves me. No, we're not getting back together. Yes, Tyler loves him and I've decided I'm willing to negotiate that situation, especially since we're going to be working together this month. Other than that, can we maybe get to the part where we have a huge town issue going on, Jonathan is trying to do something very Jonathanesque, and Noah is being adopted by the lairds?"

"Wow, I wasn't even here and I feel up to date." Spence grinned and nodded. "I guess I don't need to worry about falling behind next time I go out of town."

Lyra patted Spence's hand and grinned up at him.

Cam frowned. Vivian did not pat his hand *or* smile up at him.

He definitely had work to do.

"Vi's right. We need to regroup before Jonathan starts claiming he's an elected official." Jamie glanced around the table. "Which leads us back to... what did the lairds want?"

"I'm sorry." Spence shook his head. "Did you say... the lairds?"

"Yup."

Spence eyed Jamie like he was pulling his leg. "You know, I've been here almost a month and you'd think by now I'd just learn to say, 'Why, yes. Of course he said *lairds*.' But, alas, I have not."

"Don't worry." Lyra patted his hand again, which was starting to rub Cam the wrong way with all the affection. "You will."

"So," Cam cut in before they could actually start cooing at each other. "The lairds?"

"Backing up, for Spence." Jamie cleared his throat as if he were about to recite some big speech. "As you know, Starlight Harbor is where a collection of clans from several small coastal villages of Scotland escaped to rebuild their communities during the British assaults and such. So, from one rocky coastal fishing culture to another. They found this land, nowhere near anything else, and settled in. Insulated themselves as much as they could. Really, it was only in the last few generations that we even became accessible to the outsiders."

"Like me," Spence threw in.

"And me." Noah reached out to give him a fist bump of brotherhood.

"Right, outsiders unite... If I could continue?" Jamie waited until he was center stage again and went on. "So, the clans came here, secluded themselves—which was nothing new since where they'd come from was a remote coast, difficult to get to—and basically remade their lives just as they'd been. That meant that even though it had been several villages, they had to become one town. Obviously, each clan still turned to its own leaders. And so the lairds formed a sort of panel, for lack of a better word, to handle things democratically."

"I'm sure that always went well." Noah's eyes rolled so far back that Cam thought he might pass out. "I mean, Starlight Harbor is pretty much a drama-free zone."

"Noah, please hold your sarcasm until the end of my tale."

"My bad."

"Thank you. *As I was saying,* since then, the town has really been run by the lairds."

"Except for that whole 'selectmen and women and the town manager' thing."

Cam glanced around, kind of holding his breath because, even though it was generally accepted, this was something that just wasn't discussed.

"When the town incorporated, the state demanded they have a more typical town governance citing things like the history of hereditary tyranny most cultures left their home countries to avoid when forming this one. Blah, blah, blah."

"Really? Democracy is now *blah, blah, blah?*"

"Noah." Jamie gave a deep, put-upon sigh. "If you would like to use your wit and charm to tell the story, I'm more than willing to give up the floor."

"Yeah, right." Vivian snorted a bit of tea out her nose at that, then glared at everyone, warning them with a look not to even mention it.

Cam silently reached across the table to snag her a napkin and finally got his smile.

Take that, Mr. Pulls Out the Chair.

"Anyway, the town obviously did what they had to do to remain US citizens, but that didn't mean they weren't still looking to the lairds for their leadership. Most generations accept this. There's always people who don't. But things are changing here, so maybe that will too."

He sounded a little sad at the idea and Cam had to admit he liked their quirky little "back hall" way of running things.

"Which brings us to... Noah."

Oh, yeah.

"What did the lairds want?"

"Wait, I still have questions, so very many questions." Spence all but pulled out a notebook and everyone was a bit horrified he was already planning his next Starlight Harbor exposé.

"Honey, no." Lyra did the hand-pat thing again, but this time it didn't seem quite as reassuring.

With that, everyone turned back to Noah, dismissing the next great article about their town since Lyra would handle it.

"They're concerned about a lot of things. Of course, they are less than happy about the sleigh. They'd figured the town would take care of that, assumed everyone would be on the same page." Noah got up, went into the house, and came back with two hands filled with beer bottles. "Also, Ms. Angie. She is not going to like where they come down on this."

"Are those all for you?" Jamie asked as he reached for one.

Noah slid one his way. "But honest to goodness, those guys could drive even Lyra to drink."

"No, thanks." She grinned at him and refilled her tea. "But tell me more about Ms. Angie."

"If I lived anywhere else, I wouldn't believe it." Noah laughed, then leaned forward. "Ms. Angie is losing her car for two weeks. It was being impounded while the meeting was going on—that's why she wasn't there."

"Oh, these guys are crafty."

"And Captain Jack is being put in doggy prison on the town square until ten thousand dollars is raised to pay for a large segment of the sleigh. Which does a couple things."

He took a sip, leaning back in his chair while they all leaned forward.

"They figured it would just about kill Ms. Angie to see Captain Jack in a cutesy dog prison. They're going to put it up on YouTube live so people can send in money. And it's going to be probably the fastest fundraiser anyone would have come up with."

"Should we be scared the lairds understand YouTube live?" Jamie asked.

They all paused a moment, thinking that over. Then deciding they didn't want to think it over.

"Also, they figured we have an expert in our midst—Cam, they had some incredibly flattering things to say about you, although McPhee is still a little miffed about some ball game eleven years ago." Noah looked at Cam like he was going to dive into the history of his high school record, then shook his head. "Their feelings that the town meeting was more than a *let's all get on the same page and start moving forward* situation were, shall we say, becoming extreme."

"When hasn't that been the definition of our town meetings?" Cam asked and they all turned and looked at him. "What? I love those things. I try not to miss them. I'm ninety-nine percent sure the people from *Gilmore Girls* were secretly recording us for decades."

Noah just tilted his head to the side as if trying to figure out what *that* meant.

"Moving on." Noah took another sip of his beer. "They were shocked—as we all were—when Jonathan was suddenly on the stage giving himself a new title and announcing he was in charge. They were annoyed when he started challenging Cam from the stage. But they were ticked off when the officials just let him do it."

"So was most of the town," Jamie tossed in.

"Right, but they see this as a precedent that can't be allowed to go on. The town has worked a certain way for centuries and the fact that one snotty man with an insane ego is going to try to change it for a power grab against the kid he bullied for years is a bridge too far."

"I told you we should have kicked his ass and nipped this in the bud." Jamie pointed his beer at Cam. "We wouldn't be in this situation now."

Cam gave him a look of utter disbelief. "We were seven. You wanted to kick his ass and 'drop him off the pier' when we were in second grade."

"See? I was ahead of my time."

"Yeah, if we wanted to be mob bosses."

"Anyway," Noah stepped back in. "They had one very big concern. And I have to say, I actually agree with them."

Vivian nodded and glanced around the table. "What? You aren't all thinking it?"

"No, honey," Cam tested out the endearment on his tongue. It didn't feel right for grown-up Vivian like it did when they were teenagers.

Also, she looked like she was going to smack him.

Noah gave her a smile, and Cam considered punching him. Where was all this violence coming from?

"They're concerned—and I'd say rightfully so," Vivian started, "with the fact that Jonathan, while working in the capacity of town accountant—"

Jamie snickered.

"—apparently has a client who is unilaterally making decisions about major town events. Free of the town governance and the lairds and a vote."

She looked pretty pleased with herself and a spurt of pride went through him. People had always just seen the model's body and face with the flash of cool-fire red hair and assumed she had fluff for brains.

Nothing was further from the truth.

Man, she must be tired of proving herself over and over again.

"You know, that caught my attention, then I just put it away." Jamie saluted her with his beer. "Nice catch, Breck."

"What did the lairds say about it?" Lyra asked.

"Nothing I'm going to repeat, but let's just say they weren't happy."

"Don't like giving up control, huh?" Spence asked.

"Don't like the idea that someone from the outside may have paid off Jonathan with nefarious reasons." Noah paused and drank. "Except they did not use the word nefarious. So, Vivian is spot-on. That was their primary concern. The rest, they figure, is just details. Cam is literally a nationwide renowned expert, so he'll take care of that. They're more than happy with Vivian taking care of the internals and—" He raised a hand before she could jump in. "They realize you have your own workload. They want to know if you want town-sponsored help or to have them handle shifting some of the jobs."

Cam glanced at Vivian and could see this all running through her head. The woman thought lightning fast.

But he also saw fear and uncertainty clear as day and wondered if the others saw it as well.

"They also realize," Noah continued, "that you've worked incredibly hard to overcome some barriers because people can be jackasses and they're more than willing to throw their weight behind you during and after this project since you've proven yourself to be an incredible mechanic and businesswoman."

"I need to think about it," Vivian said, which just went to show how smart she was.

Cam would have felt like he needed to make a decision right then and then probably made the wrong one. Now that he'd made a name for himself, he only wanted to think about his art and could make people wait.

Vivian had to think about running a business.

Man, she was smart.

He grinned at her like an idiot.

"Why are you grinning at me like an idiot?"

See? So smart.

"I'm just always impressed with your business savvy. Maybe you want to run my business too?"

Vivian snorted. "You couldn't afford me."

"So, what's the plan?" Jamie glanced around the table.

Cam knew him well enough to know an hour of sitting over tea and beers probably felt like four weeks to this guy.

Noah sat back and glanced around the table. Cam feared he knew what was coming.

"They've suggested we might be able to figure out who this client is and why Jonathan thinks he can just take town power because of it."

Lyra sat up straight. "Like a mystery. We're going to solve a mystery."

"Actually..." Noah gave her a smile, the kind that only Lyra got from pretty much everyone. "I was thinking, Spence is going to solve a mystery."

"Me?" Spence sat up straighter for a second, glancing around to see if everyone was as surprised as he was.

"You. Congratulations, you've just become two new things. An investigative journalist and accepted by the lairds."

Cam glanced at Spence, who had the stupidest grin on his face. He wouldn't even try to guess which one of those things was more important.

"Okay, I can do that." He was already on his phone doing who knows what.

"You two." Noah shifted back to Cam and Vivian. "Are you able to get this done in two weeks?"

Vivian glanced at him, prepared to let him answer first.

"Here's the thing. I can get it done. And Vivian can get it done. But I'm not going to promise that date as art recovery is more important than having our schedule uninterrupted."

He glanced at Vivian who was nodding along with him.

"And," she spoke up, "there's going to be a lot of situations where only one of us can be working at a time. We need to plan for that."

Noah nodded along, putting some notes in a notebook he usually carried at work.

"Okay, we'll go with that for now."

"Wait." Lyra slapped a hand down on the table. "I don't have a job."

Spence wrapped an arm around her and pulled her in. "Don't worry, I'm sure I'll need some cultural interpretations and an undercover spy no one will see coming."

Cam grinned at the two of them, picturing the day Vivian leaned into him the way Lyra leaned into Spence. That day was coming, he was sure about it.

On that note, they all stood and headed out.

Cam watched Spence grab a coat to throw over Lyra's shoulders as he went to walk her home and grinned.

Vivian was just reaching for the door when he opened it for her.

"Walk you home?"

13

VIVIAN

IT WASN'T LIKE she could say no since they literally lived in the same building. But she'd seen him watching Spence and Lyra all night and just knew he was scheming.

She was desperately working to come up with a plan to avoid walking the short distance home with him when she remembered Tyler needed to be picked up. It was the first time she'd left him somewhere instead of having a babysitter come in, so it had taken her a second.

And now, she let out a brief sigh of relief.

"Sorry, not heading home. I've got to pick Tyler up."

"Oh." Cam lit up like a new headlight. "Perfect. Mom said she was going to make more cookies. I should swing by before she gives them all away again. She does that to torture me, you know? Claims to have made my favorite cookie, then gives them to anyone just walking by. I'm pretty sure it's her way of forcing me to stop in as if I'm not there enough."

When they got to the top of the hill, they both turned right instead of left.

Cam's solid steps matched hers perfectly without

either of them having to adjust their stride. In high school, they'd walk together, his arm slung over her shoulders, with matching gaits. If they were out of step, she'd do a little hop-skip so they were on the same foot and everything just ran like a combustible engine with its pistons all in sync.

It had always felt so natural, something that had seemed in her teen heart to say, "Yes, see? This is right."

Now it felt like every red flag she had: Run! Don't trust! Look for an escape hatch! Don't lean in. You can only depend on yourself!

It took her a block to realize Cam was actually talking.

"And so, I was thinking," he continued, and hopefully, she'd tuned back in at just the right time, "that with us working together, on the same project, it's a good time for Tyler to get to see some of the other side of woodworking. But, you know, with your guidance there."

When he paused, she said, "Oh," because she was trying to catch up.

"Right," Cam went on as if that had been some type of agreement. "There's a lot that goes into both our jobs besides the fun, physical stuff. This is an opportunity for Tyler to do some of the boring stuff. I have *hours* of reviewing old photos and sketches and comparison work with what we're left with now. Also, we'll probably want to look at doing some restoration and things like that. Take care of the entire situation at once."

He looked at her expectantly, so she nodded as if she knew exactly what he was thinking.

"He'd be like a junior intern, doing a lot of crap work, and honestly, I'd probably give him some busy work to get his art skills moving. I was about his age when I picked up my first sketchbook."

"Right," she put in because she didn't think she was agreeing with anything important yet.

"Great." Cam looked too pleased with himself.

Darn. She'd obviously misjudged the conversation.

"Wait, what did I just agree to?"

Cam stopped walking, his head tilted to the side as if he were trying to figure her out. Again.

"To Tyler being my apprentice for the at least research part for the sleigh."

She stared at him and tried to think of a reason, a good reason that was fair to Tyler, to say no.

But every time she did, she saw the excitement shining in her son's eyes when he'd taken off those huge protective glasses to look at the wood Cam had been handling.

He had a passion.

He had one of the best wood artists of this generation next door.

He had a mom who loved him.

She sucked in a deep breath, setting aside every personal fear she had about her and Cam and said, "Okay."

Cam all but did a happy dance.

"This is going to be great. Tyler's going to either fall in love with art or hate it and you'll never have to worry about him being a starving artist again."

Yeah, like that was her worry right now.

He was nine.

"We'll see how it goes."

"And we can work on this stuff in your office. You've got that big window that looks into the garage, so you can keep an eye on us."

It was exactly the right thing to say and yet a cold rush of fear pushed through her. All day, every day, Camden in her office, with her kid, watching her get all oily and...

Wait. No. She didn't care what he thought she looked like. This was her. This was how she looked.

She *cared* about proximity.

Not saying she was going to cave. She wouldn't. She'd been down that road before and knew it led to heartache.

She looked up at him, his soft brown eyes holding way too much emotion for a conversation about training her kid in a craft.

Darn it, she was totally going to cave.

No. No, she wasn't. They'd had their time and it had been a sweet first love, but he'd blown it.

He took her hand and she gave it a pull, trying to get loose. When she couldn't, she decided to let him keep it because they'd look more ridiculous fighting over her hand than the gossip she'd have to deal with later from every single person on the town square tonight.

He grinned to himself and turned them back toward his parents' house and walked on, incredibly quiet.

Which was suspicious.

But she wouldn't question it as it let her zone out and not accidentally agree to anything else.

As they walked up the path to his parents' front door, he steered her around to the back. His mother stood in the kitchen window, looking down until the automatic lights flicked on and she glanced out to see them, a smile spreading across her face as her gaze dropped to their hands.

Cam opened the back door and motioned Vi through. Before anyone could say anything, Vivian was already making proclamations.

"I'm holding his hand because it was that or beat the crap out of him and leave him bleeding on the town square because he wouldn't return my property—my hand—to me."

Both of Mrs. Ross's eyebrows rose right up into her bangs, but the smile stayed.

She opened her mouth, but out of the corner of her eye, Vivian saw Cam give a shake of his head and she shut it right back closed.

"Tyler was a joy. Harry wore him out. They watched batting videos, then went out and used the batting net. Then he showed him his new fishing lure collection he's creating. I think Harry could have kept going, but Tyler basically passed out. We put him in Camden's room, dead to the world."

It was Vivian's turn to open her mouth and then shut it.

That was a lot.

And because she tried to be a fairly aware mom, she realized today had basically been all about Tyler squeezing in as much male bonding as he could. She flashed back to all his talks about camp. So many of them were about the coaches or the camp counselors. Sure, he talked about his guy friends, but she wasn't so blind as to not spot the pattern that was growing before her eyes.

Maybe getting to spend time with Cam on the historic research would be good. Well, for Tyler at least.

She might have to have some tough conversations about where Cam fit in their lives, but that was better than just depriving him of the male role model he was obviously out there searching for.

His next step would be to become aware of it himself and place a billboard in town somehow.

"He can stay overnight if you'd like." Mrs. Ross sounded so hopeful that it almost broke her heart to say no.

"I think I should take him home. He wasn't expecting to wake up somewhere new, so it seems like maybe not the best idea."

And she wasn't sure she was ready for him to wake up somewhere new that wasn't a friend-sleepover situation.

The first time, she'd been up the entire night, waiting with her cell in hand, just in case he needed her to come get him.

Spoiler, the next day he'd had the time of his life and she was exhausted.

After a moment, she added, "This time."

"And, Vivian," Mrs. Ross said, laying her hand over Vivian's where it rested on the countertop. "I would really appreciate it if you called me Bev. You're an adult and making me feel like I'm nearly dead instead of still a decade away from retiring."

She gave a light laugh and squeezed Vi's hand. "I know you left when you were young. Maybe I'm frozen in time when you were sixteen, but you're a woman now. One of the most independent, strong women in this town. And so, I'd like us to meet as women instead of a child and an adult."

"Oh." Vivian shifted, but at the same time, she completely understood. There were people who would always be like, *Listen, young lady, I'm your elder*—even when they were eighty and you were sixty.

And then there was Mrs. Ross—Bev—who was just standing there saying, I see you, you're a grown woman who deserves the respect of being treated like one.

Vi blinked. It had been *such* a day.

"I'd like that, thank you."

Another quick squeeze of the hand, and Bev was looking up at Camden coming in, Tyler still asleep and half over his shoulder.

"Wow, it has been a day." Vivian realized she was

echoing her own thoughts. "He's sleeping like he's still four."

"Mom, we're going to take the Toyota. I'll bring it back in the morning."

"I'll be here." She went up on her toes and kissed his cheek. "You're a good boy, Cam."

Vivian tried to shrug it off, but he *was* a good boy —er, man.

14

CAM

CAM DROVE them home and raced to get Tyler lifted out of the car before Vivian could beat him to it. No way was he giving up his chance to tuck him in.

She didn't even argue, probably because it meant she didn't have to haul his sixty pounds of dead weight up the stairs. But she opened door after door until Cam was settling him down, taking off his shoes.

It was literally the best thing he'd ever done in his life.

He turned around, and there she was. Standing in the doorway, the light from the hall putting her in silhouette.

So he did what he'd been wanting to do for over a year.

He crossed the room, reached his hand out to her face, and let his thumb slide down the sharp angles of her jaw, then lowered his mouth and kissed her.

It wasn't what he'd pictured the kiss would be like. He still remembered those hot, desperate kisses of their youth. Instead, it was soft, sweet, testing. He was afraid to push, afraid she'd come to her senses and sock him a good one.

The brush of lips, over and over, as she leaned forward just enough for him to feel the yearning she claimed wasn't there. Her hands came up to his chest for an instant and he feared she could feel the crazy beat of his heart.

After a moment, afraid to break the spell, Cam leaned back, unable to even smile in his shock, and said, "See you tomorrow."

———

CAM WOKE UP HAPPY.

Not that he didn't typically wake up happy. He was a cheerful guy with a good life. But today he woke up aware he was happy.

Yesterday had been the absolute best.

It had also been a hot mess of destroyed art, town dysfunction, and apparently he now lived in a BBC whodunnit where his best friend was expected to foil the town's evil civilian's plot.

But the other stuff? That had been awesome.

Yeah, so he hadn't been doing the wooing right at first. Following Spence's lead was the wrong idea. Lyra and Spence were very different people.

But forcing her to hold his hand—that was pure them. She'd look back on it fondly one day. They'd be eighty and he'd pretend to force her to hold his hand in front of their great-grandchildren and she'd just give him that look.

And the moment he'd opened his old bedroom door and seen Tyler passed out there, his old bear sitting on the pillow at his head, Cam had nearly burst into tears.

He was such a mush.

But they'd driven home and Cam hadn't given Vivian a chance to even wake Ty up. He'd just told her to go unlock the house and he picked him up and carried him right up to his bed.

God, he loved that kid.

Nothing could make him not love that kid.

His heart had about burst.

And that kiss. He could barely bring himself to think about it because dwelling on how incredible it was to hold her, even for a few moments, made it seem like a dream—like he'd wake up and find she was still this untouchable goddess across the yard.

So no matter what, today was going to be an absolutely incredible sequel to yesterday.

Soon he'd get to work on a piece he'd never anticipated ever getting to touch—even if it was for crappy reasons. Also, time with Tyler and Vi. Best day ever.

He all but sprung out of bed like a cartoon character.

Before he headed over to Vivian's, he had to get some things in order, make sure his workshop was organized and cleaned out for this project. Today he'd get that bowl his mom requested completed for a friend's birthday gift.

There was so much to get done, but they wouldn't rush it. The town could go one scheduled guest weekend without the sleigh. They'd come up with something else great. Maybe create a Santa's Workshop the kids could visit instead.

He pulled his phone out and texted Noah that idea since he was probably already inundated with the lairds at his café.

Noah texted a thumbs-up—because he was chatty like that.

Now Cam could go make that bowl.

He hopped down the steps to his workshop, unlocking the three locks on the barn-door-style entry before sliding it wide open. He took a deep breath, letting the scent of wood and poly and freedom fill his lungs.

Man, he had a good life. Guys his age joked about living the dream, but he really was.

He took a hard look at his space. Before when Tyler was here, he was always under very direct supervision. But he might in the future be under mostly direct supervision. There may come a day Cam needed to shift some stuff around. Tape the floor with safety guidelines and such.

But for now, the idea of working in Vivian's office was perfect. It was going to be a great bonding experience all around.

And he could watch her working on engines.

Honestly, men who had a problem with capable women had something wrong in their brains. He could watch Vivian do whatever it was she did all day. He had no idea what made a car go after "turn the key." But she was just so darn capable.

He'd loved that even in high school. They'd been such equals.

Jamie had loved the girls who were all, *Ooooohhhh, Jamie, look at your muscles.*

That looked really tiresome even at fourteen.

Cam grinned to himself. He couldn't help it that he'd picked the perfect girl practically since birth.

He sorted through some stock he'd put aside for projects like this until he found what he wanted and got his tools set up.

He had things moving, a happy buzz on—pun intended.

Wood puns were the best.

If he could get this done and the first protective coat on before Vivian came to get him, that was really the only thing that couldn't be put aside.

Never break a promise to your mother.

―――――

"WHOA," a voice came from the entryway of Cam's shop. "This is flipping amazing."

Cam closed his eyes a moment, wondering what idiot had walked past all of those Do Not Enter, Danger, and Please Ring the Bell signs he posted between his small shop out front and his workspace.

Come to think of it, the shop wasn't even open. This kid had come through his private entrance to his home and walked into his workshop.

What in the world?

He turned around, pulling his gloves off as he did to study the young guy in his doorway.

"Can I help you?" Cam took another calming breath as he asked, patting himself on the back for not phrasing that as "What the heck are you doing here?"

"Yeah. I'm here about the internship." He stepped farther into the workshop, obviously not deterred by Cam's glare any more than he had been by the multitude of signs. "This place kicks ass."

"Yes, there will be ass-kicking in here." Cam took another breath and decided maybe Vivian's habit of counting to ten would help him.

He got to four before he said screw it.

"Name four pieces Raymond Havester did for the state of Maine," he said, trying to stay patient even though this guy was here ruining his flow.

He stared at Cam a long moment before opening his mouth.

"But I was told it was a done deal." He waved his hands around the area, trying to signal not just the internship but pretty much... what, Cam's life?

Cam steered him back out to the private entrance.

"You failed. Big *F*. Your effort score is awful too, but I'll give you a *D* for coming up here. Now get out of my space, or I'll hit the speed-dial button to my deputy."

Cam turned to head back inside, relieved when he heard the crunch of gravel as his uninvited guest walked in the other direction.

Before he reached the door, the kid had to open his mouth one more time.

"Whoa, who is that? And what do I need to do to get an internship working under her hood?"

Cam turned so fast he probably created centrifugal force.

"You will get off my property while showing some respect. Vivian is a flipping Valkyrie."

He almost grabbed him by the arm, but instead, he stood, arms crossed as the kid crawled into a hand-me-down BMW and pulled out, waving a gesture at him he was glad Tyler wasn't around to see.

Cam was really not sure what he was going to do about this whole hot mess he was trying to negotiate if this was Jonathan's version of sending their best.

His best what?

Saboteur?

Seriously the best thing that could happen to Cam is if Jonathan would marry someone who lived in California and move there. Forever.

"What was that all about?"

Vivian stood next to him, a weird look on her face.

Cam shook his head and pointed at the taillights which were completely ignoring the stop sign.

"That?" He tried not to growl. "That's my intern. When Jonathan said he had money to hire people, apparently, he decided to keep the money and send me some kid who thinks he's here to save the world and doesn't even know who Raymond Havester is."

With a huff that would make his granddad proud, he turned and stalked back inside, looking forward to getting back into his groove.

Cam had finally gotten back to work on his bowl. It took a while to refocus on his craft what with the idiocy he had just witnessed. But he was thankful to be at it again. Just as he started turning the bowl, the lights over his door flashed.

He waited for them to flash a second interval, letting him know it was someone he knew, his parents, the guys, Tyler, or Vivian ringing his bell.

When it didn't, he grabbed his phone and checked his Ring camera to see a young woman standing at the door. Under her arm, a portfolio swung slightly as she bounced on her toes.

A strong urge to turn the lights out and hide under a table pushed through him. But at least she waited at the door, so he figured he'd give her a shot since he gave what's-his-name one.

He set everything aside, again, annoyed now to be almost finding his groove only to have to stop—again.

At the door, he took a deep breath. The hot Jonathan-made mess and the guy who just left were not her fault. He'd be polite. He'd run through the steps, then he'd see her on her way.

Smooth as silk finish.

"Mr. Ross?"

Oh man, was he suddenly that old?

"Cam. Just Cam."

"Hi! I'm Emiko! Emiko Miro! But, um, you can call me Emi. My friends call me Emi. Man, I'm nervous. How am I doing? Really blowing it, right? Geez. Stop, Emi, stop talking."

Cam grinned and opened the door wider. At least he was going to like this one.

"Come on in, Emi. And believe it or not, that was a far superior introduction than the last guy."

"Oh wow, he must have stunk."

Cam laughed and led her back to the conference room, watching her eyes bulge out at the workshop as they cut through. A few times her hand slipped out as if to touch something, and then she'd snatch it back.

They got to the conference room, and he motioned her through the door. He stood back and watched her take in everything, then lay a hand on the table.

After a moment, she lowered herself to look across it at eye level.

"Wow, this must have taken a good chunk of time."

Cam grinned. Finally. Some common sense.

"It was a labor of love." He walked to the edge of the table. "My dad always said, build it for the man you want to become. He was usually talking about things around the house and car engines. But when I bought this place, this is the first thing I built."

"Cool." Emi nodded, totally getting what he was saying.

Of course, his father had taken one look at it and said, "Ambitious."

He'd also said gorgeous, but that had been the second word. Because his father also got it.

"Okay, so, have a seat and tell me about what you do, where you go, etc."

"Oh, okay!" She took a deep breath as if centering herself. "I've been studying woodworking since I was twelve. I started with my granddad when he came over to live with us, making these little animals for my dollhouse which I had absolutely no interest in."

"In the little animals?"

"No, the dollhouse. The animals were awesome." She reached in her bag, pulled out a small frog, and put it on the table between them. "This is the last one my granddad and I made together."

Cam reached out for it and stopped. "May I?"

She gave a little nod and he picked up the frog, turning it in his hand.

"How old were you when you made this?"

"I would've been fourteen. You can see the places he would've cleaned it up a little, but he was big on not perfecting anything for me."

"You had a really good sense of proportion even then." Cam handed her back the animal.

"You should've seen the first version. Its feet were *huge*." She laughed at herself. "So my parents weren't thrilled about my addiction to woodworking..."

Their conversation went on from there with her walking him through her education and training.

"I have to tell you, you're one of my inspirations."

Cam snorted. Jamie probably would've believed her and got all *of course I am*, but Cam was used to being overlooked in the world of art.

"No. Really. You were my final project. I'm doing an internship after the fact because of my dual school sched-ule." She opened her portfolio to a page with a collection of small sketches.

"We had to study an artist who we'd want to work with—some people seemed to think they could do dead artists, which seems stupid since we couldn't work with them."

"So was I your fortieth or fiftieth choice before taking the dead people out."

She grinned. "You were still pretty high."

He turned the portfolio to find a study of sketches of some of his pieces. "Wow, these are great." But then he saw she'd removed handles and done a second set of drawings with them hanging on a wall. "Okay, talk me through this."

The next forty minutes flew by as she explained the adjustments she made for the assignment and he gave her some praise and corrections.

"I can't believe I'm saying this." And he couldn't really, but as she'd talked, he'd realized she was gold in the making. She'd shown the ability to research, sketch out ideas, shift those ideas, and do detail work. He'd be a fool to pass on this. "You're hired."

"Oh my gosh! I can't believe it! I wanted this so much I didn't think I'd get it!" She threw herself into his arms. "Thank you! Thank you! Thank you! You won't regret it."

Cam awkwardly patted her on the back. "Sure."

Behind him, someone cleared their throat. "I hope I'm not interrupting anything."

Vivian stood in the doorway, arms crossed, looking annoyed.

Cam's first instinct was to panic.

His second instinct was to let her wonder. Annoyed jealousy looked good on her.

"Oh! You must be Vivian." Emi rushed her and wrapped her in a tight hug. "I'm so excited to see how the mechanical and the artistic come together. Cam says you're the best. I can't believe I'm going to get to study under you both."

"Um, yes." Vivian obviously didn't know what to do with this level of enthusiasm and appreciation.

"I'm Emi." She stepped back, and reading the room, offered her hand to shake.

"Nice to meet you, Emi." Vivian said the right words, but her gaze kept coming back to Cam. "So, you're going to be assisting with the sleigh."

"Right? So excited. Did you know—"

"I'm going to stop you right there. Also, I have to get back to work." She turned to Cam and crossed her arms. "When you're done here, can you come over so we can get this party started?"

"Sure."

He watched her turn and walk out, not looking back as she made the corner at the doorway on the far side of the workshop.

"No hugging Vivian or in front of Vivian." Emi nodded as if she'd made a note to herself.

"No harm done. Trust me. Vivian needs more hugs."

"Yeah, I'm sure that's totally what you were thinking."

Cam grinned. He was going to like this girl. "Come on, let's get you settled at the inn. I'll take care of Vivian."

15

VIVIAN

VIVIAN HAD WOKEN up happy but confused. And then confused had taken over happy. And then annoyed had taken over confused.

She didn't usually wake up annoyed, which made her even more annoyed.

Cam had just inserted himself into her life like he belonged there.

She'd been annoyed last night. Okay, that wasn't the right word. She'd wanted to be annoyed. That was the problem.

But when he'd taken her hand, after she'd finally given up trying to get it back, she'd felt a heartbreak of nostalgia.

A memory, long-buried of when she'd lived in the halfway house bubbled up. She'd be doing something completely mundane, like watching a video for school, and suddenly have the oddest sensation her hand was empty. That it was missing something.

She'd tried to shake it off, but it wouldn't ease.

Until one day, she'd realized what was missing: Cam's hand in hers.

Two steps into the walk to get Tyler, hand in hand, she'd nearly burst into tears.

But she'd held it together.

And she'd held it together when his mom had made her feel so welcome.

And watching her son being safely carried in his arms and laid to bed, she'd just stood there in awe. A flash of what could have been ripping her soul from her body.

And then he came to her and kissed her so gently she'd nearly wept, afraid to reach up and touch him and break the spell.

And so, of course, she woke up annoyed.

Oh, they were going to talk about this whole him-just-magically-inserting-himself-into-their-lives thing.

Vivian was almost done shifting all the work she could out into the yard so she could clean down the garage. It had dawned on her as she lay in bed last night, absolutely *not* thinking about Cam telling her he loved her or that kiss, that she needed to degrease some spaces for them to place their tools so they wouldn't get anything on them.

Also, she just wanted some time to herself. Some time to put a little distance between her heart and last night.

Cam's emotional full-court press was new and not something she'd seen coming.

For months, Lyra had been pointing out Cam was "showing signs" he still loved her—or loved her again. Lyra thought it was awesome. Wouldn't it be great if after everything, they ended up together? Like, the ultimate first-love romance story.

Vivian had tried time and again to dissuade Lyra without crushing her spirit, but nothing got through that brain of hers. Once she'd found Spence, Vivian had sighed a little with relief. She'd thought Lyra would have all her energy focused on Spence and her bakery and none left for playing Little Ms. Matchmaker. Boy, had Vivian been wrong about that. So very, very wrong.

That thing about happy couples wanting everyone to be happy couples?

True. Very, very true.

But last night had been the first time Cam had acted on it.

And she wanted to say, get over it. You don't mean it. No one ever does.

She got it, they were sixteen and he was powerless to save her from her mom, but still. She couldn't help but think —way in the back of her mind, past every other part that knew she'd been the one responsible for her actions—that if Cam just hadn't been a "we should see other people" jerk, none of the fallout would have happened.

She wouldn't have been ostracized or attacked by her mother or moved into a freaking eighteenth-century home for unwed moms.

The whole time she just knew nothing was going to get better. She knew this was life now. But she couldn't help it if her little sixteen-year-old self would wake up from dreams of going home because Cam had come to get her.

He obviously never did.

And *of course* he didn't. He was sixteen too. Not to mention not the baby's father.

But when Charlie showed up one day, looking for some help with his garage, she'd jumped at the chance. He'd said she'd have to do the books and learn about engines.

Not one other girl wanted to do that, but she'd always gotten a kick out of how Mr. Ross could make anything work. If she'd had a dad like that, she'd have lived in his toolshed.

And then she'd had Tyler and everything changed.

One look at him just kicked all the bitterness out of her heart. She loved him on sight and suddenly realized she'd loved him the whole time.

The dreams about Cam became less frequent, less needy. More just like check-ins.

He never left her heart. She knew that.

And that's why she had to double down on not letting him play this game.

Oh, she knew he didn't know he was playing a game. But it still was. Once he set things right as he saw it—won her back, made things "right" between them, supported her and Tyler in some way—he'd realize they weren't the two sweet kids they'd been a decade ago.

And she couldn't take that heartbreak again.

So, avoid, avoid, avoid.

And also, get Tyler up and ready for camp.

When she headed back upstairs, Tyler was already munching on his cereal, *Percy Jackson* open in front of him, his Thor propped up next to it.

"Ready for camp today?"

"Yup. I can't wait to show Mikey my new moves. Mr. Ross is an awesome coach. I hope he helps out today." He kept going on about baseball and Vivian didn't want to interrupt one good thing for another, so she waited until he petered out.

As he rinsed his bowl and was about to go get his backpack, she stopped him and motioned to the chair at the table.

Slouched shoulders let her know he remembered last night's promise.

"You broke your promise to me, lied to Cam, then tried

to make up a reason it was okay instead of owning those two things."

The slouch deepened, but at least there was no *yeah, but...* coming out.

"And part of me wants to say no to what I'm about to offer you because it feels like rewarding you for lying and breaking the rules. The offer comes with a punishment."

"What if I don't take the offer?" he asked, looking all smarty-smart.

"Then you just get the punishment." Geez, this kid.

"Oh."

"Yeah. Trust me, there's a punishment no matter what and you're darn lucky I didn't tell Cam the truth. Which is you don't deserve a reward for misbehaving."

"Uncle Cam?" Oh, he perked up at that.

"Yes. The deal is that Cam is going to be working on the sleigh and you can be his research assistant. He's warned me it's a lot of boring work looking at pictures and stuff, but you two would work in the garage office on the prep stuff for the sleigh."

Her son lit up like it was Christmas for real.

"The punishment," she continued, "is that you will come back here, straight from camp, and start cleaning the garage. And I mean, heavy-duty cleaning and degreasing. There will be chemicals, you will wear a mask, and you will be exhausted when you're done. This will happen for the next three days or until Cam says there's enough space for him to work on the sleigh without it getting grease, dirt, or oil on it."

"Oh."

Yeah.

"Two hours a day, working with me in there and then, if you want, you can go work with Cam after."

She half expected him to try to negotiate, she could see it in his eyes. Cam was right, he'd been bitten by the woodworking bug and even a harsh punishment wasn't going to stop him.

Obviously, *she'd* be doing most of the cleaning, she knew this. But the idea he had to and the effort were what was going to count.

"Okay." He looked up, looking remorseful. "And, Mom, I'm sorry I broke the rules. I won't do it again."

If only that were true. He rushed off to get his backpack and then gave her a tight hug before heading over to the rec center.

After he left, she went to Cam's to check on how they were going to get things moving.

Sure, he was a great kisser. And yes, she liked holding his hand. And, okay, maybe she wasn't as over him as she wished she was—wait, she'd leave that part out.

But the point was, she'd made up her mind. She wasn't riding that emotional roller coaster again. Obviously, she hadn't set good enough boundaries, so she'd have to do that. Clearly. So he understood she wasn't kidding or unsure or playing hard to get.

He'd respect that.

Cam was, above all things, a respectful person.

But she couldn't get herself to let go of the feeling he'd left her and grown-up Cam was still trying to make it right.

She was surprised to find the workshop already open, and when she didn't hear anything dangerous sounding going on, she cut through where she spotted the lights on in his conference room.

She stutter-stepped to a stop at the doorway as a pretty, younger woman threw herself into Cam's arms.

He wasn't exactly pushing her away.

What the heck was this?

After a moment, she cleared her throat. "I hope I'm not interrupting anything."

They both turned to look at her as the girl shifted away, but Cam left his arm draped over her shoulders.

He looked... amused? The jackass.

"Oh! You must be Vivian." Suddenly her body was being attacked by a small spitfire of energy. She just kept talking and Vivian got the idea she was supposed to be... helping?

"Um, yes."

"I'm Emi." She finally let go and offered a hand.

Vivian wasn't really sure what happened after that, just that she escaped the room as quickly as possible.

What was that snake doing cuddled up to his intern the day after he'd kissed her? That was just not cool.

Oh, they'd be having a word about this. Just let his cute little butt walk itself over to *her* space and she'd have some things to say all right.

She stormed across the courtyard, into her garage. After last night he'd nearly convinced her to give him a chance. Ha. Like she was going to do that. She grabbed a rag and degreaser, then started in on the tool bench she had taken everything off of last night.

Well, see? She was right, she told herself.

He was just looking for things to be okay between them again. Show that he could have her if he wanted to.

Now that he'd seen she wasn't shutting everything out of her life like Lyra accused her of on a regular basis, he was all Mr. Flirty with whoever?

And she was an idiot.

Oh, was she an idiot.

And she didn't care if none of this sounded rational

outside her head. Lyra would get it. Skye would point out why she was acting "erratic," which was a very Skye word.

But it's how she *felt*.

She was scrubbing at the counter so hard she didn't even hear the footsteps sound behind her.

"I think that spot's clean."

So he was just going to walk into her garage and say whatever he wanted? Huh?

Why was there never a handy wrench to throw when she needed one?

"Oh, are you done with your *meeting?*" She didn't even bother to turn around because there was no sense throwing a rag at him.

She was just so mad. She'd thought she'd known how she felt, and then, *bam*. Having everything thrown in her face like that showed she'd underestimated her feelings.

It was herself, really, she was upset with.

Hadn't she just been saying she *knew* she still had feelings for him but that she couldn't fall to them because... well, exactly this.

She needed to protect herself because she needed to protect Tyler. They were a unit. And they needed to be a safe unit.

"Actually, the meeting went great."

"I bet it did," she muttered under her breath.

She heard him come closer and turned, figuring she was probably starting to look ridiculous.

"Vivian." His voice was soft, but she could hear the amusement in it. "What are you doing in here scrubbing your way through that perfectly good bench top?"

"Nothing." She shot back, then pivoted. "It has to be clean before we bring in the sleigh and a place for you—and

Emi—to put your tools. We don't want to add to any of the damage."

He stepped closer and took the rag out of her hand.

"Do you want to talk about it?" he asked.

"About what?"

"About why you're grumpy." He grinned and stepped closer.

"I'm not grumpy. I'm busy. Unlike some people who apparently don't have anything to do while I'm literally cleaning a special place for them."

"They appreciate the cleaning and will lend a hand because they know this is a team effort." He slid another step closer.

"I'd rather you went and did whatever you need to do to start work."

"Maybe cleaning is what I do before I start work."

She sighed, completely exasperated.

He took one last step, right into her space at the tool bench, and reached past her.

"Can you hold this?"

Without thinking, she automatically put her hands up and he settled a toolkit weighing a good fifteen pounds into them.

"Perfect. Thanks."

Then before she could ask what he was doing, he leaned in and kissed her. Again.

If she'd thought she'd romanticized last night's kiss with the nostalgia of first love... well, she was probably right about that.

But if she thought that's why it had been so darn hot, she was more than a little mistaken.

It was so darn hot because Cam was an amazing kisser and they had chemistry off the charts.

She'd only kissed two guys since Cam. Kevin Baines and a date she went out on because the man kept asking and Charlie insisted she couldn't live her life in the past or as only a mother.

But it definitely wasn't inexperience making her toes curl.

She felt Cam's hands come up to her face, the rough callus of his thumb running gently along the edge of her jaw. His mouth slid over hers, a shocking lack of urgency as she felt her heartbeat rise and rise and rise. But the warmth of his mouth as he slid hers open was a shock and a comfort.

She was sucked in by the gravity Cam naturally had, just leaning into that heat, to that mouth.

She pulled back, and before she could say anything, he took the toolbox out of her hands, set it down, kissed her on the cheek, and said, "Thanks. I'll see you in about an hour," then strolled out.

She stared after him, a bit flabbergasted at what had just happened.

CAM HAD BEEN EXPECTING Vivian to storm over and ream him a good one for the hand-holding and the kissing from last night. But the timing could not have been better.

The flash of jealousy on her face had been priceless.

Then *she'd* realized she was jealous, and instead of telling him off for the night before, she'd stormed back out.

Vivian in high emotion—any high emotion—was a sight to behold.

And, my goodness, that kiss.

She had to see they were meant to be. That he wasn't playing around.

He went back into his workshop, back to being absolutely happy with his life—deleting that little matter of tossing that kid out this morning—and finished the bowl for his mom.

Then he set up in his conference room with all the boxes he'd need to organize with Tyler. It would be easier to figure out what was in them here and leave the extra stuff behind when they brought them over to Vivian's office.

Then he'd—

"You can't just keep catching me off guard and kissing me like that."

He glanced up to where she stood in his doorway, feet braced, arms crossed, and he fought a grin.

That had taken a far shorter time than he'd anticipated. He'd thought she'd fake indifference for at least an hour.

"You don't get to just come in there and kiss me."

"That doesn't seem fair at all."

"What?" She threw her arms open wide as she asked.

"I mean, you're allowed to come in here and kiss me whenever you want. That seems very unfair the rules don't go both ways."

"But I'm *not* coming in here and kissing you whenever I want." She practically stamped her foot as she said it.

"Well, that's your decision. I mean, you're allowed to and if you want to..."

He let the sentence fade out as if the answer was obvious.

And to him it was.

"Cam." She took a deep breath, wearing the face she wore when dealing with Tyler in a particularly petulant mood. "Let me rephrase this so we're clear. You can't go around kissing me—anywhere. We're not getting back together. We had our time, and it was lovely, but that was the past."

Cam nodded along. He understood exactly what she was saying.

"Right. I agree."

"You do?"

"Absolutely.

"Okay..." She drew the word out in doubt.

"I want you to know what I agree with." Cam waited for her to nod before he went on, sure he had her attention. "I agree we're not the same people we would have been if we had stayed together in high school."

She smiled. "Right. Exactly. I mean, more obviously for one of us than the other."

"Maybe more obvious, but equally as true. Losing you shaped me as a man in a way keeping you wouldn't have."

"Oh."

"I also," he went on before she could add some Vivian-type commentary. "I also agree we can't build a life based on who we were as sixteen-year-olds. Actually, I don't think most people can do that."

"Right."

"We've gone down paths we couldn't even have seen at sixteen. We're completely different. We're versions of ourselves we wouldn't have, couldn't have imagined. And even if we had, well, the versions of us now don't match the versions of us then. Like, your path went way wide one way and mine went narrowly another. There's no corresponding couple because we didn't walk it together."

She nodded slowly, as if seeing those paths making them into what their sixteen-year-old selves probably would have thought was incompatible.

"And I understand your—" *Fear* was the word he thought, but knew her too well to say it out loud. "—concern about me romanticizing you, us, our youth. And maybe I do. But, Vivian, you've been back over a year now. I know *you now*. I know this version of you. And she has me in awe constantly."

Vivian was shaking her head and had taken a step back.

"When I said I was still in love with you, it wasn't an ongoing thing. It was an again thing—but realizing that somewhere, in my heart, there was a bridge that reached back to the past and linked those two loves."

She took another step back.

"You can keep saying no, that I'm just trying to fix the past or regain that first love or all the other things you think, but I know one thing."

He paused, letting her take it all in.

"What?" she nearly whispered.

"I know I never found anyone to love after you left, and I'll never find anyone to love like who you are now. Waiting isn't a big deal, as long as you and Tyler let me be here, be part of your lives while you figure that out."

He watched her take one more step back, knowing he'd said everything, every possible thing he could to lay his heart on the line.

"Cam, there's nothing to figure out." She took that final step back. "You weren't there when I needed you. You left and then you weren't there. I don't know if I'll ever be able to get past that."

She blinked quickly like she was trying to hold back tears. "I can't risk my heart again. Especially like this. With you."

He froze. He thought she'd been coming around. That it was just a normal sense of fear exacerbated by the idea she didn't want to risk Tyler being hurt too.

But this was deeper than that. His blood turned to ice. What if he couldn't fix this? Maybe it just wasn't something in his power.

"I know we were sixteen and I get that to you that feels young but..." She looked like she was going to cry, and he just wanted to do anything in that moment to make it better. "But while you were young... I'd just become an adult who was still a kid. I grew up the moment I realized you—that *anyone*—wasn't going to sweep in and save me. The moment I realized I was on my own. And that someone else was going to depend on me soon."

Oh, this was so much worse than he'd allowed himself to imagine.

"And I know that's not your fault. I get that. But you were all I had to hold on to and you weren't there and... I don't think I can get past that. Even after seeing the man you've become."

She stopped, a hand raised to her mouth as if she could take all the words back or maybe just everything that had happened in the past.

"I need you to respect that."

Then, before he could form a thought that might make any of it better, she turned and sprinted out of his workshop, leaving behind nothing but a silence he didn't know if he could overcome.

17

VIVIAN

VIVIAN HURRIED THROUGH HIS WORKSHOP, blindly making her way outside, and then froze, unable to figure out what to do next.

She turned, knowing she couldn't be here, not in their shared space, and just started walking. She hadn't even known where she was going before ending up three streets over, in front of the house she'd grown up in.

She'd avoided the whole block since returning to town, but now she stood there, staring up at the house, and all she felt was thankful to have gotten out of it.

Even with years' distance, she couldn't pull up one decent memory to lean on and say, "See, it wasn't all bad."

Every positive memory had been outside that house.

"Hi there." A woman came out on the porch and smiled at her. "Can I help you?"

Vi shook her head and tried to smile. "No, ma'am. It's just... I grew up here and I haven't been by it in years."

The woman immediately looked uncomfortable.

"Oh, you must be Vivian Breck."

Vi started at the fact the woman knew her name. She knew it was a small town, but this seemed a bit odd.

"Are you here to sue us?"

"Sue you?"

"Yes, the neighbors all say you should sue us to get your house back, but we bought it fair and square."

Nothing with her mother had ever been fair and square, but that wasn't this woman's fault. And not only did she have zero interest in suing them, but after nearly two years, you'd think the woman would realize that.

"No. I don't want your house." When the woman scowled at her, Vivian's anger started to come through. "I wouldn't step in that house if you paid me. It's all yours, bad vibes and all."

And without even feeling bad about it, she turned and stormed back up the street.

She was just storming everywhere today. So she went to the one place she knew she'd be safe.

Lyra's bakery.

Starlight Cupcake was rocking, so she circled behind the counter, took two cupcakes, and went and sat at the table in the kitchen area Lyra kept for herself.

On a pass by, Lyra plopped a glass of iced tea in front of her, dropped a kiss on her cheek, and kept going.

Ten minutes later, Skye showed up.

She sat down, cup of coffee in hand, and just sipped away, not saying a word.

Finally, she spoke up. "Lyra's better at this stuff."

Vivian finally broke out of her own mind. "No. It's nice just having you here. You always settle me. You have a..." She waved her hand around, looking for the right word. "I don't know. I'm not a woo-woo person, but you have an energy about you that makes me feel safe and calm."

Skye looked down into her coffee and smiled.

"Tell me about you and Cam." She said it as a gentle directive, like this was an interview, instead of asking Vi if she'd like to tell her.

"Cam is... a great guy. Like, one of the best, right?" she asked, half hoping Skye would say, *Well, actually...*

"Yes. I've always found him kind and dependable."

Vivian smiled. High praise from Skye.

Except.

"I guess that's the thing. I couldn't depend on him. He let me down. I get it." She waved a hand as if Skye was going to interrupt her like anyone else would have. "He was being stupid, we were sixteen, he expected to get back together, etcetera, etcetera."

Skye nodded and sipped her coffee, all patience.

"But then, after everyone found out I was pregnant, still nothing. And then my mom shipped me off to that home and still nothing." Vivian felt like crying. She'd needed her best friend. She'd loved him so much, but he'd been her best friend too.

"So, you're angry with him?"

"No. I mean, I get it."

"Right. We can understand stuff and still be angry." Skye took the cookie Lyra set in front of her as she rushed by, broke it in half, and slid part over to Vivian.

"What should he have done?" Skye asked, completely non-judgmentally.

"I don't know. Maybe even just come fight with me, show me he cared a little. Show me he was *there*." Vivian burst into tears over something she hadn't cried over in years. "He wasn't even there."

"So are you afraid he wouldn't be there now?"

Lyra rushed through and pulled the oven door open.

"Everything okay in here?" She looked at Vivian and tried to give her a smile.

Skye waved her away.

"No. I mean. I don't think so. Like you said, he's the most dependable man I know."

"But still...?"

"Right, but still. How do you forget something that was so pivotal not just to your relationship but to your whole life? He did *nothing*."

Literally—in both the good and bad sense of the word.

"I understand." Skye sipped her coffee. "What would you have liked him to have done?"

Vivian sat with that, knowing with anyone else she could start listing off ridiculous, overly emotional answers. But with Skye, she lived too much by truth—both because it's what she thought was right and because it's who she was.

"I don't know. I guess just... be there?"

She sat back in her chair because she knew the answer was heartbreak and lack of trust and abandonment issues and whatever else a good therapist would call it.

But she didn't think it was fair to expect her to divorce Cam from Cam.

She wasn't asking anyone to separate teen her from adult her—not that anyone had anyway.

"He didn't even say goodbye."

Skye reached out and touched her hand. "Yeah. That hurts."

It really did.

18

CAM

HE STARED at the door for what felt like hours thinking she'd come back, thinking maybe they could work this out. Hoping beyond hope it wasn't really over before it even began for them.

He thought back to that time and of course kicked himself in the rear again for having broken up in the first place, but still. He wasn't sure what else he could have actually done.

This was it though.

He went back to his bowl but just couldn't get himself to even pick it up. He couldn't picture making a gift for someone while feeling so defeated. He wasn't a woo-woo person, but he believed in bringing joy and positivity to his work.

He set it aside, needing to get out. To get some air. He locked up the workshop and started walking, not sure where he'd end up.

He had a lot to think about and most of it was around what to do now. He'd thought his future was just a matter of winning Vivian back, but now he knew that was not going to happen...

He could keep pushing. She might eventually cave. But that seemed cruel. To both of them.

And to Tyler.

She had a point about Tyler and him. But, man, he loved that boy. He didn't think he could love him more if he were his biological son. Could he step away from Ty?

Not if he stayed here. Not if he was in Starlight Harbor. And that was the crux of it.

He loved her. He loved them both. He'd been building a dream of a family in his head and she... what? Did she tolerate him? Was she hurt when she saw him? Did he make her think of her stolen childhood and abusive mom?

If any of those were true, then that made the decision easier.

It was one thing to leave because he was being hurt and stubborn. If it was just because he couldn't have what he wanted, that seemed childish. If that was it, maybe a trip to study with the Highland artist who was creating gorgeous dovetailed chairs would be a good break.

Focus on something new.

Before he could change his mind, Cam pulled his phone out and emailed the contact Alex McGregor had given him when they'd met two summers ago at a retreat. There was no sense putting off the ask, and he felt better just knowing he'd reached out to see if that proverbial door was still open.

Then he'd play it by ear and come back when he was ready. When he could just be her friend. When he wouldn't want to die every moment of every day when she met someone else.

Of course, he didn't think that time would come, so he might have to come up with a different measuring stick.

His feet eventually led him to Noah's café. He wasn't sure how he even got there, but as soon as he walked through the door, he knew he was in the right place.

"Cam!" Noah grabbed a mug and motioned to the end of the counter where there was an empty stool across from where Noah had his ever-present notebook open.

Cam sat, wrapped his hands around the mug, and stared past Noah.

Man, he was going to miss this guy. It was amazing how quickly Noah had become like another brother.

And as much as he loved Jamie, he also could predict what he'd say: *Chin up, Cam. She'll come around. Just keep at it.*

Only that's obviously not what Vivian wanted. She'd been clear and that was all that mattered. He had to respect that.

"So." Cam cleared his throat and Noah stopped to glance his way, giving him his full attention when he got a good look at him. "I'm going to be... um, doing some traveling here in a bit."

"Really?" Noah's voice was carefully neutral.

"Yup. There's this guy I've been wanting to study under in Scotland. I shot him an email this morning. So, you know. I'm going to need you to..."

Cam waved his hand around as he didn't have the words for "Watch out for my family and Vivian and Tyler and that my workshop doesn't get burned down and everything I love and keep them safe."

"Yeah." Noah nodded. "Of course."

"Good. Yeah, good. Thanks, man."

"Right, so." Noah pushed one of the cookies Lyra sent over each morning for him to sell his way. "How long you thinking? Couple weeks? A month maybe?"

"Probably longer than that."

"Oh, like a semester abroad. I wanted to do that. Did the Army instead. Still abroad, but people occasionally shot at me."

"Yeah, I'm not really sure. Maybe... let's just say it's open-ended."

"Sure. Got it." Noah slid him another cookie, then gave a head nod Cam just caught out of the corner of his eye.

"Stay as long as you want. Maybe we can grab dinner after this?"

Cam thought about everything he had to do before he left, but Noah was on the top of his people list, so he said, "Sure," and went back to scrolling through wood videos on his phone with his cookies.

"Hey, Cam." When someone clapped him on the back, he turned to find all three of the lairds standing there. "Not starting work yet?"

"Oh, hey. Apparently, we can't touch it until the insurance people get here today."

McPhee nodded. "Makes sense. But we couldn't help but overhear you saying you're taking a trip."

"Yeah. But not until this is done. Then I'll be heading out. Scotland."

They all murmured their approval at that.

"You're moving on, then? Off into the big world?"

Cam nodded and looked down into his coffee. "I might have the chance to study under some master craftsmen."

"Cam, correct me if I'm wrong, but aren't you a master?"

"Well, yes. But it's good to keep growing your art. They do some really interesting things over there I'd like to learn."

"Mm-hmm."

Cam put on a polite face, wishing they'd just leave already.

"Well then, that sounds good." McPhee sat down on the stool next to Cam as the others leaned against the counter. "Heard one of the interns wasn't a complete idiot and you took her on. And we wanted to let you and Vivian both know no matter what was said at the meeting, you don't have to have this done by the next weekend. We stressed the value of the cultural icon over the stupidity of needing it too fast."

Cam nodded. He appreciated that, but the urgency to get it done was one of the things he appreciated about the hot mess since it was guaranteed to get him out of town faster.

"I was thinking," he said instead, "what about a little workshop. The kids could come in to see Santa. They could do a spiel about being busy year-round or something."

All three men nodded.

"We're already on it. Noah let us know about your text and that was better than any idea we'd come up with."

"Good, good." Cam didn't want to be rude to his elders, but he really just wanted to get back to his brooding now.

McPhee gave him a hearty slap on the back again and they all moved down to the end of the counter where they stuck their heads together with Noah.

After a few moments, Cameron came back over and asked, "Anything else you think we should know?"

He didn't think they were asking about his personal life, so he answered, "No, sir," and really honestly hoped they'd just move along.

"Everything is working out fine with you and Vivian?"

Cam's head came up and he narrowed his eyes, wondering why the lairds would bring up Vivian.

"What do you mean?" he asked suspiciously.

"You guys are going to have to work together on the sleigh. I'm sure it's going to be a tough schedule. We want to get her part done as quickly as possible so she can get back to work. She's had a rough time getting that business of hers up and running and we want to make sure to protect that."

Cam didn't want to be here any longer than he had to, but he also didn't want to damage Vivian's business in any way.

Maybe now was a good time to go up to Bangor and do a review at Raymond Havester's estate. It couldn't hurt to see if they had anything on file that might help. Get him out of Starlight Harbor for a week or so.

"I'm sure we won't have any problems working together," he said instead.

Even he could hear the bitterness on the end of that sentence. Of course they wouldn't have problems working together. It was just everything else he had problems with.

"Cam, look at me."

He raised his eyes to finally look Cameron in the eye and saw something not unlike regret.

"Son, you do what you need to do." He gave a tight nod, then said, "Don't do anything rash," and turned and walked out the front door.

And if that wasn't even more ominous than what Cam had been dealing with, he didn't know what was.

19

VIVIAN

AFTER HER TALK WITH SKYE—WHICH was surprisingly good—Vi walked back to her shop, thinking about that last question. What should he have done?

Skye seemed to understand it didn't matter what he could or couldn't have done. It mattered that Vivian felt deserted and thrown over when really, Skye was right. What could he have done? That she was living with a mixture of still live heartbreak and a deep fear of being hurt again. Especially by Cam.

Skye had even pointed at the twin—Lyra had given only one of them a second chance—and said, "Vivian, that's how old you were when this happened."

She looked at the sunshiney girl, all happy and bubbly even as Lyra worked her behind the counter, and thought, *My goodness, I was a baby.*

"And..." Skye looked a little nervous to say the last part, bracing herself as if Vivian might attack her. "That's how old Cam was too."

She watched the girl flit around, flirting with a boy in a

windbreaker from a different school who'd obviously come in to walk around and hang out on the square, and thought *point taken*.

She could work on rewriting her emotions about the past, but she couldn't promise anything. And if she were being honest with herself, she thought all it might do is allow her and Cam to be back on equal footing as friends.

Which was the best she could ask for right now.

She'd been surprised when the Cameron laird had driven in and invited himself to inspect her garage, asking if she needed anything. After a few moments, he gave her an odd look of surprise.

"Well, there's your Camden."

Vivian watched Cam stalk back into his workshop, the waves of emotion practically radiating off him as she muttered, *not mine*.

He literally started whistling innocently.

Uh-huh.

"Can we just get back to this?" She headed back inside feeling overwhelmed with what was going on. And so far, all she'd done was show one of the lairds around the shop and office. He seemed pleased with what he saw, which was good if they were going to trust her to back the sleigh in here and take care of it.

They'd made promises to Noah that she had to believe were true. She couldn't risk everything she'd built on the whim of old men though.

"Sure." He grinned like a man who knew something. Everyone thought they knew something. "Most of what I came by for was to make sure you understood we support you and whatever you need to do to make this work. Like I said, Forsyth's nephew has been wanting to move up here for a while now, but he couldn't find a job. Most of the garages in the area don't like to hire outside their family."

Vivian snorted. "Yeah, no kidding. I'm shocked to hear it."

He paused as he was pulling out his little planner, realizing what she said.

"No one ever considered you an outsider, Vivian."

Really, this is when he wanted to do this? In the middle of a business negotiation.

It dawned on her the amount of power currently in her hands. They knew how she worked, that she did a lot of the older cars in town because she hadn't updated everything to computers like the Youngs had when they'd expanded to open shops outside of town. They'd seen she could listen to an engine and hear what it was saying. And of course she had a good setup for Cam to do the work he needed right here as well.

And now was when they suddenly felt the need to make sure it was clear she *wasn't an outsider*.

"Maybe not," she finally answered. "But that might make it even worse."

Because if this is how you treated family, then she wasn't sure she wanted to be that either.

He gave her a sad nod.

"Vivian," he began, his entire demeanor changing. "This has been on my mind for years and I think one of the reasons they sent me to clear everything with you was because I've been the one sympathetic to your cause since you were a kid."

Oh geez, he really was going to do this right now.

He noticed her stiffen and raised a preemptive hand.

"It's always bothered me, but the others argued that we

stayed out of family business." He turned and took two steps toward the window at the back of the shop as if he couldn't meet her gaze. "I was new to my position. My grandfather raised me and held his seat until he died. When he had just passed on, he was eighty-seven. Which I was decades younger than the others and still unsure what power I had—if any."

She gave a nod, not surprised to hear any of that and oddly believing he felt some regret.

"Then they told me the Rosses had taken care of it, so I felt a little better. Figured you were safe as houses and let them have their way."

He shook his head as he stared at the ground, the remorse rolling off him in a way that made her want to comfort him.

"I understand, sir. These things happen." It was something she got used to saying to a lot of people when she turned up pregnant, but she found herself meaning it this time.

He gave her a sad nod and didn't add anything, but there was something he'd said she had to understand.

"What did you mean when you said the Rosses were taking care of it?"

His head came up, apparent surprise on his face. "You mean you didn't know?"

At the shake of her head, he went on. "Harry and Bev came to us just as everything was becoming public. Let us know they were having you move in with them. They knew there'd be gossip but their family had already decided."

Vivian stood there in shock. She never even heard a whisper of this.

But Cameron wasn't done.

"They had some concerns obviously. The first one was

your own mother, but they figured she could only backpedal so much once you were under their roof. The town would have to deal with her raising a fuss though, so they felt like they should let us know just so we could be prepared. Harry made it clear he expected us to be standing behind them and they'd take the reins once you moved in."

"So." Vivian stepped away, her gaze searching the room for something, anything to latch on to while she rocked through these revelations. "Why am I just now hearing about this?"

"We agreed. If she did something stupid like contacting the state—let's just say our community has had centuries of maneuvering around outside bureaucracy."

That did not surprise her.

"The Rosses had everything lined up and were going to go speak with your mother then. We were going to send McPhee over with them in an attempt to make things go as smoothly as possible. But when they got there, they were shocked to find you were gone."

Vivian remembered the day vividly. Her mother had packed her a small suitcase, not even everything she would've packed herself for a trip, and had it in the car when she got home from school. She took Vivian's phone and told her she had five minutes to grab anything important she may have forgotten. Next thing she knew, Vivian was in a sponsored home outside Boston.

From there to Charlie and it was years later before she even considered reaching out to Lyra.

Because she was an emancipated minor, she was able to finish her time in the home and then move in with the closest thing she ever had to family to complete learning everything he could teach her in the garage.

Even super pregnant, she'd been working on cars.

He laughed that it brought in more women customers.

When Tyler came along, it was just the three of them.

And as crazy as it sounds, it was some of the best years of her life.

Charlie loved her and Tyler as if they were his own and in their reality they really were.

She was grieving when she came back to Starlight Harbor. It just wasn't for her mother.

"When your mother came back from wherever she took you, we couldn't pressure or cajole the location out of her. I think Bev nearly threatened to burn down her house and only didn't because she couldn't go to prison since they were in the middle of finals."

Vivian laughed. She could see Bev making the decision consciously not to burn down her mother's house.

"And if any of the kids knew where you were, they weren't sharing. Then your mother died." He said it so casually she knew he was trying not to make a thing of it.

And the saddest part was, it really wasn't.

Their relationship was something Vivian feared she'd replicate with her own child.

Her mother was never actually physically abusive and as a kid she thought that mattered. But emotionally? Absolutely. And maybe fiscally or security-wise? Vivian didn't know what the word was for withholding things like a full meal or new clothes for school.

She pulled herself back out of her memories as he continued.

"And I guess none of us were really surprised to find she hadn't left you the house." He shook his head as if he couldn't believe it, a flush rising up on his neck. "Okay, I'll admit it. I couldn't believe it. I figured at the end of her life she'd do something to make up for the type of mother she'd been to you. But when the town found out she had donated it to a nonprofit we couldn't work around..."

Vivian remembered hearing about it as well. She hadn't expected her mother to give her the house, but she'd always wondered why she hadn't just sold it. And now she began to realize it was because her mother put more faith in the town to be a good parent than she herself wouldn't.

And she wouldn't risk Vivian even getting that one thing.

"The others thought you would come back as soon as she was gone." He shrugged "I didn't think you'd come back at all. I figured you'd had enough betrayal in your life."

He turned to face her fully and took a step in her direction.

"So when I tell you the town will have your back, I'm making you a personal promise. Not from the town. Not from the lairds. I'm making that promise from me. Because I figure that's the least I owe you."

She still had so many questions, but they were running through her head too quickly to put them into words.

It just wasn't something to discuss now.

But she had a feeling if she ever went to Cameron in the future and asked them, he'd be more than willing to answer whatever she came up with.

"And—" He flashed her a grin. "My car has never run better since you came back. You're not just the good choice, you're our best bet."

He patted her on the shoulder, obviously not expecting anything from her right then, and headed out.

She watched him go, feeling a little pride that yes, his '72 Mustang did run better than since she'd moved back.

What was a girl to do when she discovered everyone she thought had let her down, had had her back?

She couldn't wrap her mind around it, so instead she went upstairs to get lunch ready for Tyler.

And to continue avoiding Cam while she readjusted all her thinking.

20

CAM

CAM HADN'T ANTICIPATED how much he would need to consider when moving to a different country. The fact his invite came about an hour after he sent the email was flattering to say the least.

He had no idea how long he'd be there, but he suspected it would be quite a while.

He wasn't stupid enough to say until Vivian was out of his system because he assumed if he came back, even after years, his heart would still ignite at the sight of her.

He doubted there'd ever be anyone else for him but her. But he also knew he wasn't someone to marry for anything less than this fierce love he felt just at the thought of her.

That might mean being alone for the rest of his life which nearly knocked him over with a sad pang. He thought of his parents and how they'd been together for what seemed like forever. How they were a couple and best friends and a team.

He'd always pictured himself having that one day.

Maybe he was wrong. Maybe as he aged and *he*

changed, he'd find that since he and Vivian hadn't grown into something together, he'd find something else that made him love like he'd hoped to grow into loving Vivian.

But he doubted it.

Glancing around his workshop, he figured there were a couple things he'd want to ship to Scotland. There were tools that were fit to his hand and no loaner or new version would be worth the hassle. He didn't want to give up everything he built just to get away, regroup, maybe find a new way to mend his heart.

The workshop would be closed. He'd already made a list of things that need to happen.

First on the list was to finish that darn bowl for his mother.

Everything else would have to take care of itself.

But some things would not take care of themselves. And he was not looking forward to this part.

He locked up his workshop and headed over to his parents' house.

There had better be cookies after all the stress of the day.

Reaching the door, he heard his mother and father laughing together in the kitchen before he went in to join them. It reinforced his decision. He was doing the right thing, and not just for Vivian, but for himself. There was no way he could live a happy life always being on the outside with her and having to be careful about his words and his actions. Maybe even how he looked at her.

Because she had asked him, in sincerity, to back off.

And so, because he loved her, he had to.

"Hey!" His mother turned and smiled at him as she handed his father another baby tomato plant. "Look who's here, and it's not even mealtime."

His father laughed and slapped him on the back as he walked by with the plants to set them on the back porch.

"Hey, parental units." He closed the door behind him. "How goes it?"

"It goes. What brings you by? Need up to your room for more research?"

"No. I wanted to talk to you both." He slid a chair out and motioned for his mom. Instead, she grabbed the pitcher of tea off the counter and his dad grabbed three glasses before they settled around the table with him.

"So..." Cam cleared his throat and glanced around trying to figure out how to say this.

It wasn't like he was dying. But he was afraid that's what it would sound like since that's what it felt like. "Some things have come to light, an opportunity has come knockin', and I'm here to get you both up to speed."

"Oh." His mom looked nervous and he hated that. "I was hoping you were stopping by to tell us you got a dog."

Cam stopped, replayed every conversation he'd had with his mother for two weeks, and couldn't figure out where that came from.

"A dog?"

She shrugged. "I guess it just seemed like the next step. We'd love to have a dog to watch occasionally."

Oh. Family, grandchildren... dog.

This was already going worse than he'd expected.

"So, no. No dog. But I do have some exciting news." His mother practically started bouncing. "I've been accepted by McGregor to study under him. It's something I always considered the next part of my career. So I'll be heading over to Scotland as soon as the sleigh is done. I'll get a chance to really dig into a different set of mediums and a new specialization. It's a great opportunity."

His parents paused, looking confused before his mom spoke again.

"What about Vivian? And Tyler?" She probably didn't mean for her questions to sound like an accusation, but they definitely felt like it.

"So, that's kind of... off the table. This seemed like a good time to take some time and..." He really should have written a script or something on his walk over. But he'd spent the entire time thinking about their reaction, not his telling.

"What do you mean off the table?" his dad asked, wrapping his hand around his mom's.

He knew they'd take his leaving hard since there was no end date, but he had underestimated how attached they were to Vivian and Tyler as future Ross family members.

He took a long sip of tea, trying to not bring his own pain out too much to explain it.

"Vivian has asked, clearly and politely, for me to let her go and not reissue my campaign to win her back."

His parents stared at him. His dad collapsed back in his chair while his mom reached out and wrapped her hands around his big one resting between them.

"So, Scotland?"

He nodded, glad they understood immediately and weren't going to make it a thing when it was hard enough.

He forced a grin. "You'll have a wonderful time visiting."

"How long?" his dad asked.

"Until I'm sure I can come back and be here and keep my promise."

His mom got up and came around the table, her eyes already damp with tears she was trying not to let fall.

"Camden Frazier Ross, you're one of the best men I know." She kissed him on the cheek and headed out the back door before either of them could start to cry.

21

VIVIAN

VIVIAN SCRUBBED AT ANOTHER WORKBENCH, her mind whirling with the clash of what she had known to be true an hour ago and what seemed to be true now.

She didn't know if it changed anything. She still wasn't sure if she could change the years of heartache and fear at what she had believed had been *true*. As true as if it had happened because in her heart and mind it *had* happened and she'd had to live with the fallout alone for years.

People expect you to learn a piece of information and for your life to change. For you to be like, *Oh, wow. My entire late childhood and adulthood were framed wrong and everything I believed wasn't true, so POOF, let me just change everything now.*

She'd watched a documentary on leaving a cult once, and she couldn't help but wonder if this is what it felt like.

To believe two clashing things at the same time, knowing only one was true.

At least she knew she could count on Cam to finish this job and to work with Tyler while he did it. He wasn't the type of guy to say, "Oh, you aren't interested in me? Okay, forget this job and forget your kid."

If anything, she could count on him because of it. He was the type of man who would double down and do all the right things twice as hard to make sure she felt comfortable and there were no hard feelings.

It would take a couple weeks, but they'd be back to normal. Their group of friends was great and so solid it would be easy for them to just move on.

And honestly, now that she'd drawn a line in the sand, he'd probably find someone really quickly. It wasn't like she moved back to town and hadn't noticed all the women throwing themselves at him. It'd been kind of funny at first, watching him casually deflect all the bodies collapsed at his feet—okay, that was a little mean.

But the truth was he was always respectful as he side-stepped invitations.

Of course, it did start to get old. Didn't these women have any social temperature-taking abilities? He made it obvious pretty quickly he wasn't interested usually.

That's one thing she knew she could respect from him. She'd drawn the line and he would respect it.

Not just because he respected her, but because Cam had an innate sense of self-respect she couldn't help but appreciate.

And on top of that, she felt like their relationship would be even more positive than before.

She's always been on guard in some little way around him, even if she never felt he put her in an awkward situation.

Now that he understood where she stood, their friendship could become even more solid than it had ever been.

And she'd have no qualms about Tyler spending time with him because she could answer honestly that she and Cam were the best of friends and that's all it was, so don't get attached in any other way. But she was sure Cam would never let him down.

Sure, the whole conversation had stunk, but they probably should've had it sooner. It would've made things more comfortable for both of them over the last year.

She was just finishing up on the bench when she turned to find Noah standing there, glancing around her garage with a little bit of envy.

"You don't rent space, do you?" He stepped into the shade of the open bay. "I'd love to bring my car in here and play with you one day." He smiled and moved in to stand next to where she leaned against the bench.

Vivian gave him a bright smile. Since Noah had moved here, he'd been easy to love.

He was just one of the best people she knew.

"You coming to debrief me after another meeting with the gentleman lairds?" She couldn't help but laugh. Noah had somehow managed to land in the middle of those guys without trying.

Maybe one of them should have warned him when the older men quietly moved their headquarters into his café.

"They did have a lot to say this morning in the café. They seem to think I need a waiter so they can be taken care of and also bend my ear as much as they want."

Vivian snorted. "Yeah, I really see you hiring somebody just so you can stand around. Totally sounds like you, Noah."

"Hey, I'm not gonna lie, they do have good intel." He laughed and moved away from the bench, giving a glance around the room before turning back to her. "But that's not why I'm here."

Vivian stopped and gave him her full attention. Noah didn't typically stop by. He texted.

A rush of panic slid through her.

"What's wrong?" All the blood in her body suddenly felt cold. "Is someone hurt? Is everyone okay?"

Noah stepped forward, waving his hand. "No. No, sorry. Everyone is fine. I just..." He stopped and ran a hand over his short hair. "This isn't something I like to do, but I had to come down here. I sat around thinking about it all morning. But if you don't know something, then you won't be able to do something until it's too late, and then I'd feel bad about that."

One thing she learned about Noah very quickly, he was an absolute caretaker. Not a gossip, not a busybody, but just a straight-up caretaker.

And that's why he was stirring up a real sense of panic in her.

"Okay, you're still kind of freaking me out."

"Right. I'd like to tell you something. And I'd like it to remain between us."

"You said that already."

"Right." He nodded again. "If you decide to do anything about it, fine. But if you don't, I'd like you to just sit on it for a month or so and not say anything."

Vivian took in a deep breath. She trusted Noah explicitly and that was the only reason that, after a moment of worry, she nodded her head and said, "Okay."

He walked over to her, looked down into her face, and sighed. A very un-Noah-like move.

"Cam was in my café earlier."

"Is he okay?" She suddenly felt like anything could have occurred since they talked and she wouldn't know. What if something happened to him or his parents or...

"Vi." Noah pulled her attention back. "He's fine. He's as normal-fine as a man going through a horrible breakup can be."

"We didn't break up. We didn't break up because we weren't together."

"I understand you think that. But I also understand that our Cam believes in things like destiny. Having you say never—it's *like* a breakup to him." Noah paused. "And he desperately wants to keep all the promises he gave you. Which, to Cam, means taking himself out of the situation because he doesn't think he can be around you and keep them without making you feel uncomfortable."

She paused, realizing how true that probably was.

All her thoughts of getting back on track in a few weeks were pushed out further. Months probably. But she'd be patient with him. He was a romantic, but he was also the best man she knew. One of her favorite people. He'd come around and she'd just wait for him to do so.

"Did you come here to... what?" It wasn't like Noah to take sides or yell at anyone, so she wasn't sure where this was going.

"I'm here to give you one little piece of information." He sucked in a deep breath as if he were jumping into the deep end. "Cam is going to Scotland."

"On vacation?" That might be... good? Right? Like a little time apart.

"No. Vivian, honey. He's moving there. He's going to go study under some other wood dude and he's making plans for it to be long-term. In his mind, long-term is pretty much forever with visits back to see his family."

The blood that had been running cold froze as Vivian took the words like a punch.

"I just thought you should know."

Noah leaned down and kissed her on the cheek before leaving her standing in her empty garage in stunned silence.

22

___

CAM

CAM HAD PLANS TO MAKE. Part of him was excited and he focused on that.

He'd always been one to think positive, take the good and run with it. That's what he was going to have to do to make this work.

Not only was he being invited over to study, but they were asking him to teach a class on Americana. Of course he couldn't say no to that. He was already building the curriculum in his mind as he sorted through everything he'd have to do over the next month.

And every few moments, he reminded himself: silver lining.

Luckily, he had no need to or interest in selling his workshop or building, so while it might feel like a giant storage unit, it would be here for him when he was ready to come back.

Vivian and Tyler also wouldn't have to deal with an unknown person sharing their space. Not that there were a lot of unknown people in Starlight Harbor, but hey. Better safe than sorry.

Especially with the space he'd built this into. He could think of several regional artists who would jump at the chance to sublet if it came to that.

His mind kept skirting away from explaining this to Ty. He'd find someone to keep mentoring him if the sleigh project went well.

Maybe Emi if she was a good fit. Students could always use a job and it had to be better than the one he'd had slinging lobsters up the coast. Maybe even sublet the apartment to her if she was going to stick around.

Wait and see. He still had a month for decisions like that and wanted to make sure it was a win for everyone he left behind.

He was just putting aside one more box that could go over to Vivian's office when his phone rang. What was with this week? Every time he tried to get some work done, there was an interruption.

He glanced down and there was a number from town he didn't recognize, so he figured he should probably answer it in case it was an emergency.

"Camden, this is Selectperson McCreary. We need you at town hall."

Not a request.

Cam wasn't a fan of orders, but he also wasn't a fan of waiting any longer for this job to get moving.

"Sure. When?" Cam glanced around his office at the stacks of papers he still wanted to get through tonight.

"We were thinking how about... Now?" It was half statement, half question.

Cam let out a sigh and then felt guilty about it.

Maybe getting down there meant starting things moving. If a few questions answered would speed things along, he was all in.

And it was one more thing to keep his brain busy today while he was still adjusting to his new future.

He made some notes about where he was in his planning and work, then locked up and headed over.

As he came up the hill, he could see several other people walking over to the town buildings and had a flash of Ms. Angie trying to steal a car and make a run for it with Captain Jack so he didn't have to do doggie prison this weekend.

The jail was already being built, and he had to admit, it was pretty adorable. Two kids had volunteered to be Cat Cops for the video, and he figured they'd hit their ten-thousand-dollar goal with the under-twelve crowd leading the charge.

"Cam!" Jamie pulled up beside him on his motorcycle and cut the engine. "Heard there was a very quiet meeting happening in town."

He snorted as he took in the throngs of people heading over.

"I guess this is quiet compared to some other meetings we've had." He glanced at the bike as Jamie stored his helmet. "Couldn't help yourself?"

"Nah. Was just working on Shelly to get her all spiffy and smooth and figured this would make a good break."

They came around the corner of the town hall and stopped mid-stride.

"So, this is..."

Even Jamie was at a loss for words.

"This is a lot." He glanced around, suddenly seeing the rest of his afternoon slipping away. "Not at all a small *we could use your help for a second* situation."

"Ha. You fell for that? Selectperson McCreary uses that every time she needs something and it's never pretty. I once ended up with a prospective governor's family on Shelly for a day because I fell for it. And the four-year-old hated sailing and was seasick the whole time." Jamie shook his head in disgust as if it was the four-year-old's fault. "Maine coastal family. Eighth generation. Seasick."

"You're all heart."

"Hey, you do six hours on your boat, not getting paid, and dealing with not saying the wrong thing all day. *And* add a sick kid and a family unwilling to take the poor suffering child back to shore. What was wrong with people?"

"When have you *ever* worried about saying the wrong thing?"

"Oh, not me." Jamie smacked a hand to his chest and tried to look innocent. "I didn't care, but I knew you would, so I threw it in there."

Cam glanced around the lot behind the hall surprised at how full it was. "It looks like the whole town is here."

"Nah. Too quiet. But this is something. What do you think they want?"

Cam shrugged. "Figured it was just some questions from the insurance guys, but... I mean, this is Starlight Harbor. It could be anything."

He'd expected to have to push his way through the crowd, but as they moved forward, people just got out of their way until they made it to the middle of the excitement.

In the center, standing in front of the sleigh were two guys in suits who stood out from pretty much everyone. In Starlight Harbor, suits were for weddings and funerals... and for some kids, the prom.

These guys weren't feds, so they must be the insurance people.

The older one in the red tie seemed to be in charge. The

younger one with the blue tie looked confused to even be there.

So sorry our national treasure is too kitschy for you, Mr. Blue Tie, huh?

Selectperson McCreary stood between the suits and Jonathan on one side and the lairds on the other. Off a bit from the two groups, notebook in hand, Spence tried to blend into the crowd. He was doing a much better job than he would have a month ago.

Cam glanced at Jamie to see if he had any take on what was going on. With a shrug, Jamie took the last step out of the crowd, knowing he'd be standing with Cam.

"Camden. It's about time." Selectperson McCreary motioned to him.

Cam just stared at her since she'd only called him seven minutes ago. After a moment she cleared her throat and said, "Thank you for coming up so quickly."

"Of course." He turned to the suits and introduced himself. "I'm Camden Ross."

"Right. Mr. Ross." Red Tie gave him a nod and glanced down at his notes. "I understand you're the local artist who would like to lead the renovations of the sleigh."

The tone immediately felt like an interrogation, so Cam decided to act accordingly. And hoped Jamie would too.

"Yes." Answer the question asked.

Red Tie waited as if Cam would add something to that, but he didn't know what the guy was looking for.

"And your qualifications?"

"You haven't been given my specs page?" Cam was already losing patience because this felt like the build to an attack, not to mention a complete waste of time. Professionals had pages for this very reason. He was incredibly easy to research, not to mention the town had the entire specs page for when someone reached out to the tourist center.

"I have, but I'd like you to go over it and also we'll need to verify them."

"I'm incredibly easy to verify if you Google me. The state of Maine, the governor's office, Havester's estate, several local colleges I've spoken at, a list of state and federal buildings my pieces are photographed in… I could go on?" Cam left it as a question.

Blue Tie gave him a half-apologetic look behind Red Tie's back.

"We'll need a list of verifiable sources."

"As I stated, they're on my website."

"You can send—"

"I'm going to stop you right there. You have my info. You have my verifiable list available to you. I'm not a businessman or the owner of this sleigh. I'm an artist—a well-known, well-paid, highly trained artist who the town has hired. You do your job, I'll do mine."

From the back of the crowd, a voice shouted, "You tell 'em, Cam."

When it came to Starlight Harbor, there were guests and there were outsiders. It was obvious which group these two fell into.

Guests were something closer to visiting family.

"We'll take a look and be in touch."

Cam reached into his back pocket and pulled out an old card. "You can reach my agent here."

Red Tie looked at the card as if he weren't going to take it. Cam kept his hand out. This guy obviously had no respect for what he did, so he could go old-school on him. Blue Tie moved as if he were just going to take the card and hope to get things moving again.

"That's hardly necessary." Jonathan stepped in. "I have Camden's number if you need to reach him."

Red Tie stared at him a moment longer, then Cam tucked his card back into his wallet. "Suit yourself. I can tell you I will absolutely not be available by phone or appointment as I'll be busy. You don't want to follow standard protocol for working with artists, that's up to you. Or maybe it's up to Jonathan."

A few feet away, Spence *mm-hmmed* as if he had a lead on a big story.

"Camden, don't be a child."

"Jonathan, I'm not. I'm being a professional. I know this might confuse you, but as one of the most highly regarded wood artists in the country, I am not at your beck and call."

"Stop overestimating yourself, Camden."

Beside him, Jamie snorted. When Cam gave him a look, Jamie shrugged and said, "Hey. This *is* me trying to stay out of it."

True, very true.

Since Cam was working incredibly hard to find each and every silver lining about leaving, he added "Jonathan" to the list, and felt his lips involuntarily curve in a goofy smile.

"What?" Jonathan demanded.

"Oh, nothing. Just, you know... you."

Completely confused about what that meant, Jonathan just glared.

"You know," Jonathan finally said. "I have the power to take this all away from you."

"Actually—" Selectperson McCreary started.

"And don't think I won't," he finished.

"Again, actually—"

Jamie snorted again.

"You know..." Cam turned to Jamie. "That's not helping. Your snorting is as vicious as other people's words."

"Yes, and I worked hard to make it so, so don't deny me when the opportunity arises."

Cam just stared at him, trying not to be overly annoyed because of the level of ridiculousness they were already surrounded by.

He turned back to Jonathan, his last nerve finally hit for probably the first time in his very laid-back life.

"Let me stop you right there because you seem to be missing some very important facts. Red Tie here might want to be aware of them as well." Both insurance guys looked down at their ties and Cam charged ahead. "You are not a town official. You do not make town decisions. I am not a public servant. I am a highly trained, highly regarded artist who is doing some very expensive work at a bottom-level cost because of my love of Starlight Harbor and Raymond Havester's legacy."

Jonathan went to cut in and Cam raised a hand, surprised but not really when he flinched.

"You do not make the final decisions on anything going on here except which day you write the check you're obliged to by the council. Let's get this thing done. The sleigh got damaged, it needs repair. The town has two incredibly qualified experts willing to do so at a very affordable price. Can we finish this so I can get back to work?"

"Oh, diva," Jamie muttered under his breath with some pride.

"So—" Red Tie looked down at his notebook again, then glanced at Jonathan with obvious frustration. Apparently, the narrative had just shifted drastically for him.

And Jonathan, being only moderately socially an idiot, couldn't help but notice either.

Cam glanced at Jonathan, feeling slightly bad even if the guy had brought everything on himself.

"This is not making us look like adults."

"Sure, the town hero returns to save the day and wants to look like he's the one who takes the high road." Jonathan glared at Cam who couldn't help but wonder if this was ever going to end. "And look! He found a way for his hussy of a girlfriend to come out looking all pure and innocent too."

Cam was on top of Jonathan before he even planned to swing.

Insult him. Insult his art. Be a jerk in general.

Fine.

But come for Vivian and you might as well decide on pistols at dawn.

Cam was choosing fists at now.

He swung, fast and hard, a brutal hook to the jaw that, frankly, left him feeling surprised Jonathan kept his feet. Before he could anticipate it, Jonathan was coming in low and fast, tackling him to the ground. Instead of trying to sidestep the attack, Cam took it on, ready to finish this in the most direct, primitive way possible.

Nearly twenty years of this crap was too much and he was tired of taking the high road.

Plus, at this point, his parents couldn't ground him, so he figured he was pretty much in the clear to kick some ass.

Sooner than he'd have liked, Jamie pulled him off Jonathan and Spence backed Jonathan away from them—with very little effort reminiscent of the old "hold me back, hold me back" skit.

"You can do what you want, but this town is outdated. We need to bring it into at least the last century." Jonathan was practically spitting as he shouted. "You think your cute little committees and tours and happy-happy days are going to keep this town alive and thriving? You're all idiots."

He stood there, chest heaving as blood ran from the corner of his mouth.

"Life isn't a fairy tale and this town is a lie." He wiped the blood away, surprised to see it on his hand.

Cam just shook his head, shocked at the vitriol. "Then why are you here? You left, just like so many of us, and came back. Trust me, no one was here thinking, 'Wow, when do you think Jonathan will be back to save us from... happiness?' I mean, really. Just leave. No one is keeping you here."

Jonathan braced himself as if he was expecting another attack or was about to start one himself.

"He can't." Jamie's voice came from just behind Cam's shoulder, not a surprise since he'd always had his back. "Can you, Jon-Jon?"

Cam sidestepped to look at Jamie without turning his back on the tornado that Jonathan had somehow become.

"You came back because you couldn't cut it outside. What? No job, or maybe you got a job but didn't like being low man on the ladder? People buzzing by you—people you were as smart as but maybe just were not horrible humans to be around? There's a lot more competition outside these town limits. Especially for someone with such mundane skills as accounting. You come back here and you shine, right? Not a lot of competition for accountants."

Cam glanced back at Jonathan whose jaw was locked tighter than a Bessey clamp.

Huh, looked like Jamie was onto something.

"But then you got here and everyone was doing just fine without all that math."

"I don't know," Cam interjected. "I'm not gonna lie, I

like math. And woodworkers need math... Sailors need math."

Jamie gave him a look.

"Okay, it wasn't the math. It was the power. You thought you could make yourself indispensable to the point of control. But this town is bigger than money in, money out. And then a situation came up where you could throw your rival under the bus."

Cam could see it. If he thought Captain Jack was bribable, he'd be questioning just how the sleigh accident had *really* happened.

"If all that's true, then what does it say about you two, huh? I'm not the only one who thrives in this town."

Jamie turned, all innocent to Cam. "Did I say he was thriving? I'm pretty sure I didn't, right?"

Jonathan made a half-hearted lunge Spence managed to hold back while still making notes in his Moleskine.

"I never planned on not coming back." Cam shrugged. "I can do my art from anywhere. Why wouldn't I want to do it close to my friends and family? But... that wasn't the draw for you, was it?"

Cam shook his head. It was sadder than he would have imagined. That didn't mean he was all, "Let's throw Jonathan a party and make him part of the group" but he certainly felt a small, tiny, wee little layer of pity coat over the animosity.

Then, without realizing he was even speaking, he said, "That's just sad."

And he meant it.

He even meant it when Jonathan broke free from Spence and tackled him to the ground again, hitting him with all the aggression he'd been showing for the last two decades.

This time, there was no tearing him off Cam who found himself actually working to fight back, get Jonathan off him, and get away.

"That's enough!"

Cam was vaguely aware when the voice broke through the crowd.

"I said, that's enough."

Cam was more than happy to be done with this since he wasn't twelve anymore, but Jonathan just kept swinging. He'd reached up, pushing his palm into Jonathan's face to try to push him off when the first slam of cold water hit him.

Jonathan rolled off him to find Skye in full deputy mode with the fire department letting loose on them from a short hose.

"Jonathan Baines, Camden Ross." Skye stood over them, arms crossed, somehow looking annoyed and amused at the same time. "You are under arrest for public brawling, disturbing the peace, and at Jamie's request, being complete jackasses."

Cam snorted and rolled to his feet. He turned and offered Jonathan a hand, which was promptly swatted away.

Then, because he was enjoying himself way too much, Cam put his hands out to be handcuffed.

"What?" Skye asked.

"Cuff me."

"I don't think it's come to that."

"Come on! When am I going to get arrested again?"

"If you and Jonathan stay in the same town much longer, probably on a regular basis because I am sick of your shenanigans."

A wave of sadness washed over Cam as he realized there probably would be no more chances for Starlight

Harbor shenanigans. Unless he worked hard to fit them in this month.

Instead, he just smiled at Skye and said, "Come on. Don't be a spoilsport. I could make a break for it."

She cuffed him because it was easier than not.

Everyone turned and looked at Jonathan.

"I have no interest in being handcuffed."

There was a general grumbling through the crowd.

Blue Tie, who had remained so quiet up to this point, mumbled, "This town really grows on you, huh?"

Red Tie did not see the humor.

But Skye was walking a cuffed Cam and an uncuffed Jonathan, so Red Tie couldn't really do anything about the rest of the conversation.

They were nearly to the town building which housed the sheriff's department when Vivian came running up.

"What is going on? Why is he in cuffs? Why is Jonathan not in cuffs? Whose idea was this? I demand justice."

Skye let out a long sigh and turned to an irate Vivian.

"Justice for what?"

"For Cam! Justice for Cam!"

From behind them, the crowd started shouting, "Yeah! Justice for Cam! Free Cam! Free Cam!"

Cam's heart melted as he watched his Valkyrie fly to his rescue. Even if she'd never love him the way he loved her, she'd always have his back.

Which—just made him love her more.

Skye turned and glared at Vivian. "Do you see what you did?"

Vivian looked a little guilty but powered on. "Why is Cam cuffed? How is that fair?"

"Because the idiot demanded to be cuffed because he

might not ever get arrested again and didn't want to miss out."

"Oh." Vivian turned and gave him such a damning look that he felt oddly proud of his ridiculous insistence.

And with all the grace he had even after landing on a rock when Jonathan tackled him, he just shrugged.

"Yes, now if you'll excuse me, these two have created enough paperwork to last me several hours."

"You know," Vivian said, giving her a contrite smile. "Why don't I walk over to Lyra's and get you a few of those ginger cookies and maybe a thing of peach iced tea?"

Skye smiled at her and turned back to Cam and Jonathan.

It was exactly what Cam needed to see. Vivian, after being exiled, had made a home, a family, and a support system. Starlight Harbor was going to be good to her.

And maybe one day he'd come back and be able to appreciate that fully.

Skye marched them up the front steps and then down into the lower levels where the sheriff's offices were. He'd never been down here, but the front was really cozy if a bit sterile. He was already thinking of what he could design to make it a bit more welcoming when Skye pointed him through a set of doors. Four small cells were broken out along the old stone foundation. She put Jonathan in one, then motioned for Cam's hands.

Unclicking the cuffs, she stuck them back on her belt and looked up at him. "Happy?"

"Completely joyful."

She put them across from one another which was a relief since that meant he wouldn't be tempted to reach through the bars and strangle Jonathan with his bare hands.

She closed the door, leaving them alone. Cam sat down

on his cot, wondering who had actually spent time in here. Even the guests typically never got tourist-crazy.

Jonathan paced back and forth, obviously more upset than he was trying to let on.

"Wanna talk about it?" Cam asked, partly because he felt a tiny bit bad for him, but mostly because he absolutely had no idea how things had started or even escalated to this point.

Jonathan turned and gave him a gesture he didn't think Skye would appreciate, so Cam stretched out on his cot and figured it was probably the last bit of quiet he'd have for a while, so he might as well enjoy it.

It wasn't five minutes later he heard a raised, familiar voice.

"I demand to see my son." His mother had apparently been alerted to his situation.

He heard a low response that must be Skye.

"I don't care if you say he's fine. He was *attacked* with hundreds of witnesses. I have a video already on my phone and I'm sorry, Skye, I love you, but prisons are dangerous places."

Cam glanced around the fairly comfortable little cell with its high window overlooking the town square and snorted at the word *prison*.

"Well then," his mother responded to whatever Skye had said. "You won't mind letting me in to see him. Harry is already calling our lawyer."

The only lawyer anyone in their family had was the contract guy who did work for Cam's business, so he couldn't imagine who his dad was calling.

"Bev!" A high voice joined in the fray. "I'm so glad you're here."

"Vivian, do you know what happened?"

A low voice broke in between their rushed conversation, hushing them up. There seemed to be some type of bartering going on, but he was only getting a few words.

A glance over at Jonathan showed he was struggling to listen too.

Cam felt that same small wave of pity when he realized no one was shouting, "Free Jonathan," or demanding his release.

Not that the premier jackass didn't bring it on himself.

Finally, the door opened and Skye stuck her head in.

"You get one visitor. The ladies decided between themselves. Five minutes."

Deputy Skye was definitely every bit by the book as he'd known her to be.

He expected his mom to step through the door, but instead, Vivian pushed a Starlight Cupcake bag into Skye's hands as she rushed by her.

"Cam!" She hurried over to his cell and stuck her hands out to grab his. "Are you okay?"

"Vivian, I didn't beat him with a rubber hose and then submit him to water torture while you were at the café." Skye sounded completely offended, but closed the door and left them to it.

"I'm fine. I'm sure this is just going to be handled by the town and I'll be out of here soon. No damage done."

"It's going to go on your permanent record," Jonathan added from across the aisle.

"Yup. And one of us works for ourselves and the other one works in a role that means a background check to handle money. Hmmmmm..."

Vivian turned and glared at Jonathan. "Do you mind?"

Jonathan waved his hand in a *continue* motion and she turned back.

"I'm so mad at you and I don't even know where to start."

"You're mad because I got arrested?"

"No, I'm mad because... are you going to Scotland?"

"Wow, is it up on Facebook or something?"

"I have my sources." Vivian stuck her nose in the air and he knew there was no sense trying to figure out just who had told her.

It saved him the pain of telling her himself.

"Not until the sleigh is done. I wouldn't leave you hanging like that."

"You are such a jackass."

23
———

VIVIAN

SHE COULD NOT BELIEVE he couldn't see what a huge deal this was. As if Facebook might be the problem. Or even like she might be angry he'd leave before he'd fulfilled his commitment to fix the sleigh.

What was wrong with him?

"You were just going to leave?"

"You're leaving?" a hopeful Jonathan asked from across the way.

"Do you mind?" Vivian spun and glared at him.

"Hey. It's not like I can *go* anywhere."

She bit her tongue, partially because that was true, and turned back to Cam, who looked far too amused.

"What?"

"Right. So." Cam cleared his throat. "I am going to Scotland—"

"Yes." Jonathan all but did a fist pump.

"—but not until the sleigh is done and I've wrapped up some stuff."

"And this just magically happened today?" She crossed

her arms instead of reaching through the bar to smack him upside the head.

"Magic!" Cam said with a big grin and all but wiggled jazz hands.

You know, maybe prison was the right place for him. She'd just let Skye know to keep him.

"Camden."

"Yeah, *Camden.*" Jonathan snorted.

Vivian turned, needing to take her ire out on someone. "How long do you think Skye could forget you were in here if no one asked where you were?"

The look of terror Jonathan shot past her to Cam was very telling.

"*As I was saying...*" She turned around to deal with her primary jackass. The one who was thinking of leaving her again. "You woke up this morning and just suddenly wanted to work in Scotland?"

"You know, not *suddenly.* But after some emails, yes. That's what has happened. And..." He lowered his voice and stepped as close to her as he could get with those bars. "You don't need to do this. It's always been on my bucket list. And I'm sure, the timing is... good. But, yeah."

He ended with a head nod, and she wanted to smack him again.

"When were you going to tell me?"

Cam gave her a frustrated glare. "If you haven't noticed, I've been a little busy since this morning, arguing with Certain People and getting locked up, but it was totally on the agenda for after I took down Insurance Red Tie Guy later."

"Camden."

"Vivian."

She stepped away, paced the twelve steps to the end of the little hall and back.

"You were just going to leave." Even as she said it, she heard an echo of his words just a few days ago. That she'd just left.

And she layered that over the fact he *had* tried to stop it. He and his parents were going to go so far as to open their home to her—and her baby.

She stepped back in front of him and wrapped a hand around one of the bars.

"I don't want you to go."

"I do," Jonathan grumbled behind her.

"Hey, I was not kidding about that thing before. I was thinking Skye needs a weekend off. Girls' trip to Bangor maybe?" She pointed at him. "Do not make me take you down and keep you in here."

She turned back around to find Cam smiling at her broadly. He opened his mouth, then shut it quickly, wiping the look from his face.

"What?" she challenged him, figuring he had smartassery to say also.

"Nothing." He put his hand around the same bar, just above hers but not touching. She could feel the heat, but not the actual skin or calluses on those long, lean fingers.

"Nothing?" She was trying not to get frustrated here. "You're just leaving the country and it's nothing?"

"Well..." Cam's neck was getting red as he struggled for words. "There's no point in my staying here. I've got things to do, places to visit."

"Like Scotland."

"Yes. I'm sure it's going to be a grand adventure."

"Yup. Probably." She glanced sideways up at him. "Tyler always wanted to see Scotland."

She watched him swallow, then give a sharp nod.

"We've been saving up to do something special. Maybe we could go there too."

"It's a big country."

"Actually—" Jonathan started from the other side of the row.

"Not now, Jon-Jon." Cam's gaze never left her own.

"Or maybe we could do something when you come back," she pushed, knowing what his plan was.

Cam finally glanced away, blinking.

She let the silence grow until there wasn't another way to do this.

She let go of the bar, walked over to Jonathan's side, and waved him over. As soon as he was in grabbing distance, she snatched his shirt and pulled him into the bars. He was so surprised that he fell into them.

"You, your whole family, owe me. And because of that, you're going to go sit on that little cot over there and cover your ears and hum to yourself. Otherwise, they will never find the body with how far I will bury you at sea. Do you understand me?"

His eyes grew wide and he stared down at her for a moment. When she quirked an eyebrow, he nodded and backed away until he was on the far side of his cell.

When she turned back to Cam, he had the stupidest grin on his face she'd ever seen. And that was saying something.

She stepped back up to his side and lowered her voice again, more than a little surprised that Jonathan was actually humming and he'd picked *Poker Face*.

"I have some things I want to say to you." She waited until he nodded. "I'm going through an... adjustment. I'm finding out things that make truths from the past lies. That my beliefs about you and my own history might not be as cut and dry as I'd thought."

He gave another small nod.

"That doesn't mean I'm not scared to death of you. Literally, I think. I think loving you again could nearly kill me if it went wrong. But—"

She took a deep breath, not sure what else to do.

"But since I already love you, it's more love-you-and-hurt-alone or love-you-and-learn-to-trust-us. Both are really scary. Both could leave me broken. But I'm standing here, looking at the man you've become, finding out about the boy you actually were, and I know one thing."

"What's that?" Cam asked in a hushed voice.

"That there's no one who deserves my trust more than you and you already have my love." She watched a tear slide down her guy's cheek as he ignored it, so focused on her. "And how can I not put complete trust in a man who was willing to leave the freaking country to keep a promise to me?"

"You can't. I mean, it's a rule, right?" He slid his hand down and covered hers. "And now, look at that, you're stuck with me."

24

TWO MONTHS LATER

TWO MONTHS LATER

"SHE LOOKS GOOD." Vivian watched the sleigh go by, a fresh splash of color after the complete restoration Cam and Emi had done.

Cam wrapped an arm around her and pulled her in. "We're a good team because she sounds great too."

The six weeks working together had tested their newfound acceptance of what could be. They argued. They planned around each other. They worked together and against each other's schedules, but each of them secretly loved every moment of it.

Vivian rested her head on his shoulder, keeping an eye on Tyler where he was bopping along after Harry to get them all gelato.

"It's going to be rough with you gone for the fall."

This time they got back together by communicating and making sure the one leaving knew it wasn't over—they were never over—and to come back.

"Right? But I can't wait for you all to visit. My parents are already looking for a place for all of us and Tyler is going to get such a kick out of the trip."

And that was another thing. Vivian was still fighting herself about boundaries, but Cam wasn't pushing. Well, he was trying to not actively push.

It was obvious how he felt about Tyler, but he hadn't mentioned it. He just kept being there, being perfect for them.

She was going to miss him so much.

"And we'll video chat every day. And Emi is going to stick around to keep the shop open and work with Tyler on his drawings."

See? Just absolutely perfect.

"But." He leaned in and placed a kiss on her forehead. "Nothing will keep me from coming back as soon as I can. Nothing will ever keep us apart again. I'll always find you even if I come back and you've taken off to South America."

It was the thing she most needed to hear.

Not that he loved her, she knew that. Not that he'd care for her and Tyler, even though she could do that herself.

But that he'd never, no matter the circumstances, leave her locked out and alone again. He'd done his best before and now he was a man who would move any obstacle to get to her.

Or so he'd said.

And she believed him with her whole soul.

"You were right about something." She turned and looked up into the face she never really stopped dreaming about. "The love? It never stopped. And it never will. I'll love you until forever."

And right there in front of the town, he kissed her.

25

NOAH

NOAH CLEARED the table and watched the last couple walk out after his lunch break.

It was a nice day, one of the last before the kids headed back to school and the famous New England "Indian summer" he'd fallen in love with started to show its face. He may be a transplant from the outside, but his soul was all Maine. All Starlight Harbor.

He was just thinking of walking over and throwing the closed sign a little early, when the three gentlemen walked into the café and turned it themselves, locking the door behind them.

Where Noah had grown up, that would have signaled some bad crap about to go down.

Of course, he wasn't sure that wasn't true here too—just maybe in a more emotional manipulation type of way.

These guys were easily as intimidating as his drill sergeant.

But there was no point in dodging them. Especially since they'd just locked themselves in his café uninvited.

"Gentlemen, late-day coffee?" He pulled the pot he'd

been about to empty. Serves them right for getting the last of the pot.

"Sure." They all sat at the table they'd basically claimed as their own. "And why don't you join us."

He figured he would since he was a man who liked to face things head-on.

When he placed the four cups down and dropped into a seat, they all looked to McPhee.

"We have a proposal for you."

"That feels tinted with hues of an offer I can't refuse."

He paused before saying, "Can't might be a tad strong."

But, he noticed, not off the table.

"Gentlemen, let's hear this proposal."

Might as well get it over with.

Of course, that was before he found out what exactly they were proposing. Maybe he should have dodged after all.

———

WATCH for Noah's story and find out exactly what Starlight Harbor is going to suck him into next!

ALSO BY BRIA QUINLAN

STARLIGHT HARBOR Series

The Sweetest Things

Back to You

BREW HA HA Series

It's In His Kiss (FREE Prequel)

The Last Single Girl

Worth the Fall

The Catching Kind

The Proposing Kind

Things That Shine - A Crossover Brew Ha Ha /Double Blind
Story

Bria's YA set RVHS Secrets

Secret Girlfriend

Secret Life

And YA Standalone

Wreckless

MEET BRIA

Quirky Girl & all around lovable klutz, Bria writes Diet-Coke-Snort-Worthy Rom Coms about what it's like to be a girl and deal with crap and still find love.

Her stories remind you that life is an adventure not to be ignored.

She's an RWA RITA, RWA Golden Heart, & Cyblis nominee as well as a USA Today Best Seller, & natural blonde rep'd by the Lauren Macleod of the Strothman Agency.

Want to stay in touch? Get the latest Quirky News: HERE

Want to hangout? Check her out here:
briaquinlan.com/

Made in the USA
Columbia, SC
01 July 2023

19736010R00109